VALLEY COMMUNITY LIBRARY
739 RIVER STREET
PECKVILLE, PA 18452
(570) 489-1765
www.lclshome.org

LADIES' MAN

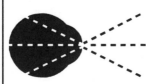

LADIES' MAN

SUZANNE BROCKMANN

THORNDIKE PRESS

An imprint of Thomson Gale, a part of The Thomson Corporation

THOMSON
—★—™
GALE

Detroit • New York • San Francisco • New Haven, Conn. • Waterville, Maine • London

THOMSON
™
GALE

LIBRARY OF CONGRESS CATALOGING-IN-PUBLICATION DATA

Brockmann, Suzanne.
    Ladies' man / by Suzanne Brockmann. — Large print ed.
        p. cm. — (Thorndike press large print core)
    ISBN-13: 978-0-7862-9190-8 (hardcover : alk. paper)
    ISBN-10: 0-7862-9190-7 (hardcover : alk. paper)
    1. Single mothers — Fiction. 2. Detectives — New York (State) — New
York — Fiction. 3. New York (N.Y.) — Fiction. 4. Large type books. I. Title.
PS3552.R61455L33 2007
813'.6—dc22   2006031020

Published in 2007 by arrangement with The Bantam Dell Publishing Group, a division of Random House, Inc.

Printed in the United States of America on permanent paper
10 9 8 7 6 5 4 3 2 1

For Kathy Lague, the Tribal Master
of all things Misty and Trek — and
owner of all notes above high C

ONE

Ellen Layne knew it was a mistake to leave the house without a book.

But her uncle Bob had insisted there wouldn't be a single moment of downtime all evening — a quick trip in the limo to Kennedy Airport, intercept Great-Aunt Alma as she began her three-hour stopover before her flight to London, dinner at one of the airport restaurants, then back home after tucking Alma safely on the red-eye to England.

They would watch the tape of last night's show on the VCR in the stretch limousine, he'd told her. And even though Ellen had already watched her legendary uncle's late night talk show when it aired, she knew he wouldn't appreciate her reading while his face was on the screen.

Bob Osborne, the king of late night television, was good at an awful lot of things, but being ignored wasn't on the list.

So now here she was, in Kennedy Airport, waiting for a flight from Chicago that had been delayed for an hour, with nothing whatsoever to read.

It was something of a fluke that they were even here. Bob was supposed to be in Boston preparing for next week's broadcast of his show from Faneuil Hall, and Ellen had an acting class that usually ran from six to nine. So Bob had made arrangements for someone else to meet Alma's plane. But then her acting coach had gotten cast in a local film and the class had been canceled, and Bob had been called back to New York this afternoon for a meeting with his network's executives, so here they were.

And Ellen was here without a book.

Bob was happy as a little clam, interrogating the security guards who X-rayed the carry-on luggage and ran metal detectors over people who set the walk-through gates abuzz. His team of bodyguards — who doubled as both built-in audience and straight men — hovered nearby.

Ellen had escaped and now headed for one of the airport newsstands, hoping they would have *something* that she hadn't yet read.

There was a book rack that held all of the *New York Times* bestsellers and then some, but what really caught her eye was the young man standing in front of it.

From the back he was a living, breathing advertisement for *Buns of Steel.* He was wearing softly faded blue jeans with a white button-down shirt tucked into the waist. His shirtsleeves were rolled up and his sport jacket hung casually over one shoulder.

His hair was blond and thick and wavy, and longish in the back, spilling over his collar. It was the kind of hair that was meant to be touched.

Ellen stood next to him and, gazing up at the rows of books, risked a sidelong glance.

He was even better looking from the front.

His profile was something to write poetry about, with a long, straight, elegantly shaped nose and an exceedingly firm chin and . . .

Oh, perfect — he'd caught her staring.

Feeling the heat of a blush on her cheeks, Ellen reached for the nearest book and flipped through it.

"That's a good one," the man said. His voice was husky and rich, with only the slightest trace of urban New York. He was even younger than she'd first thought — probably not much more than twenty-five or twenty-six.

She had probably been ten years old when he was born. *That* was a sobering thought.

She'd worked as a mother's helper when she was ten, and she'd frequently changed the diapers of a baby boy who was probably around this young man's age now. Andy Tyler was his name. This could very well be Andy Tyler standing there next to her, his diaper rash long since cleared up.

He'd turned to face her, leaning casually against the book rack with one elbow.

He was impossibly handsome, with the kind of eyes that were startling in their blueness. He had cheekbones that were as strong as his chin, giving his face a rugged, angular look and offsetting the prettiness of his elegant nose and gracefully shaped lips. There was a small scar near his right eyebrow that made him look just the slightest bit battle worn.

She was staring at him again, blankly. He'd said something to her, hadn't he?

He smiled, and dimples appeared alongside the corners of his mouth. His teeth were straight and white and as perfect as the rest of him. He gestured toward the book in her hands.

"Have you read any of his stuff?"

Ellen glanced at the paperback she was holding. *Alien Contact,* by the popular nonfiction writer T.S. Harrison. It was a fascinating collection of interviews both with people who claimed they'd been abducted by aliens and with scientists and psychologists who discounted those claims.

"Yes," she said, finding her voice. "Yeah. Actually, I've read this one already. I've read them all — except for his most recent release. Have you? Read his . . . stuff?"

The young man smiled again, and this time his eyes seemed to twinkle. Lord, he was good-looking — and he knew it.

"Every word of every book," he said. "He's one of my favorite writers. But I'm prejudiced. T.S. is a good friend of mine. I know him pretty well."

Ellen flipped the book over, but there was no picture on the back. There was never a picture on the back of T.S. Harrison's books. He never made public appearances, never put his face in the spotlight — never showed his face, period. "Really? I've heard he's something of a recluse."

"No, he's just careful about his privacy." The young man grinned. "I think he's afraid some head case is going to come after him with a gun."

"I don't blame him." Ellen thought of the security system installed in Bob's town house. The place was like a fortress, made complete by his staff of highly trained and highly paid bodyguards. These days celebri-

11

ties couldn't be careful enough.

"Are you coming or going?" the man asked, his gaze skimming briefly down her body, taking in her sleeveless silk blouse, her slim-fitting skirt, her tanned legs, the soft leather sandals on her feet.

Ellen couldn't believe it. He was checking her out, his gaze lingering just long enough on her curves and her legs to make sure that she knew he appreciated what he saw, but not long enough to be rude. And when he met her eyes again, she saw a definite spark of interest and attraction.

But he'd just asked her something. Was she coming or going? It didn't quite make sense.

He picked up on her confusion easily — no doubt he was a pro at reading women's body language — and explained. "We're in the airport. Most people are either coming in or flying out."

"Or waiting for a delayed plane to arrive," she said.

"You too, huh?"

She nodded.

"Waiting for your husband's flight?" It was a loaded question. He was fishing for information.

Ellen was flattered. And amused. And intrigued enough to tell him what he wanted to know. "I don't have a husband. At least not anymore."

"I'm sorry. When did he die? I figure he's got to be dead — or insane. No one in their right mind would walk away from a woman like you."

Ellen had to laugh. "Does that usually work for you? I mean, it's such an obvious line."

"I can be more subtle if you like."

The look in his eyes was anything but subtle. But, still, Ellen couldn't take him seriously. This was just a lighthearted flirtation, a casual chemistry experiment. He was bored and she was available as a distraction.

But she was bored too — or at least she had been, up until about three minutes ago. She glanced at her watch. Another thirty minutes before Alma's flight came in. She had plenty of time, and there was definitely no harm in flirting. Even if he was much too young.

And it had been years since she'd let herself look into a handsome man's eyes and fantasize about the limitless possibilities — and known that he was fantasizing the very same thing.

"I definitely like subtle," she told him.

There was a flare of something in his eyes. Victory? Excitement? Amusement? She couldn't tell.

"You're not a native New Yorker," he said. "I can tell from your accent. Or rather, your lack of accent. Where are you from?"

"Just Connecticut."

"Are you here in the Big Apple for just the day, or . . . ?"

"For the summer."

"Only the summer?"

She nodded. Her kids would need to be back in Connecticut when school started in September, but she didn't want to tell him that. Her baby son, Jamie, was going into eighth grade. And Lydia, her daughter, was going to be a high school sophomore. It probably hadn't been more than seven or eight years since this man had been in high school himself. "I've always wanted to live in New York," she told him, "so I took the summer off and . . . here I am."

"Greatest city in the world," he said. "You can come to New York and behave as outrageously as you want — within the confines of the law, of course — and no one will even take notice. There's a real anonymity in the crowds."

"That was very subtle," she said. "The behaving outrageously part."

His dimples appeared again. "Thank you. I thought so too. And as long as we're on the topic — do you like going to art museums?"

"Not really. In fact, not at all." Ellen gazed at him pensively. "I'm not sure I get the connection. Outrageous behavior and art museums? Unless maybe you have the habit of doing something in art museums other than looking at the exhibits."

"Actually, in my opinion, art museums are the opposite of outrageous, so it's a negative connection. Art museums tend to be nonthreatening and well lit — and that's a perfect first-date ambiance. See, I could ask you for your phone number to make a date to go to an art museum, and you might actually give it to me. The art museum approach tends to work a little bit better than the truth."

The look in his eyes was making her heart pound. She knew she shouldn't push it, but she couldn't resist. After all, she had no intention of actually giving this man her phone number, to go to an art museum with him or not. It didn't matter how charming and handsome he was. "And which truth would that be?"

The dimples deepened. "I don't know — give me a few seconds to come up with a good answer."

"I can't believe you're not ready with a

snappy comeback."

"That's because I have this overpowering urge to tell you the real truth — that the combination of your perfume and your smile is hypnotizing."

"So much for subtle."

"I lied," he admitted cheerfully. "I'm hardly ever subtle and I hate going to art museums. Besides, subtle doesn't seem to be working too well with you, so I'm going to switch to the direct approach." He held out his hand. "My name's Sam, and I'd love it if you gave me your phone number."

Ellen hesitated only for a fraction of a second before she slipped her fingers into his. Sam's hand was warmer and much larger than hers, his fingers and palm slightly callused. It was a nice hand, a strong hand, a not-at-all-subtle hand with blunt-tipped fingers and short-trimmed nails. She liked his hand. She liked his name too. Sam. It suited him.

"I'm Ellen," she told him. She gave him a smile instead of her phone number.

He held on to her fingers even though the handshake had long since ended, lightly stroking the tops of her knuckles with his thumb. "Ellen, if you give me your phone number, I promise when I call that I won't ask you to go to an art museum."

"I'm sorry, I really can't." Ellen gently pulled her hand free, turning back to the book rack. "So, what do you recommend?"

"Dinner at a supper club, with lots of slow dancing."

She shot him a look. "You're a natural for *The Dating Game.* I *meant,* what do you recommend to read?"

"Oh. I guess . . . anything by Grisham."

"Done that."

"I know. How about a romance?"

"Ooh," Ellen said. "Another flash of subtlety."

"I'm still trying."

He may have wanted her phone number, but he was also being careful not to stand too close and not to appear threatening in any way. She liked Sam, she realized. His sense of humor seemed solid, and his smile was off the scale. And those neon blue eyes. Talk about hypnotizing. She could imagine how heavenly his arms would feel around her, slow-dancing to some old, familiar song . . .

The airport loudspeaker cut through her reverie. "Paging Ellen Layne. Will Ellen L-A-Y-N-E Layne please come to the information desk immediately?"

"I'm sorry, they're calling me — I have to go."

"Without giving me your number?"

"Sorry, I can't. It was nice talking to you." She started toward the door, determined to be strong. It would be certifiably insane to give her phone number — *Bob's* phone number — to a stranger she'd met at the airport. And add into that equation the fact that Sam was ridiculously young . . . "I *am* sorry," she said.

"Okay, then I'll give you mine." He fumbled in his jacket for his card.

But she didn't have time to wait. And she didn't want the temptation of this man's business card, tossed into the bottom of her purse where she could reach in and get it and dial the number in some sudden moment of weakness. "I really have to go right now," she said, backing away. "It *was* nice meeting you."

He gave up searching and followed her to the door. She turned, picking up her pace, half hoping he wouldn't chase her all the way across the airport and half hoping he would.

"Look, it's easy to remember — 555-2356," he called after her. "The numbers are in sequence, just skip the four. I'm in the 212 area code."

Ellen couldn't resist looking back.

Sam wasn't following her. He was standing in the doorway of the newsstand, watching her walk away. "Call me," he mouthed, miming a telephone with his hands. "555–2356."

She tried to fill her mind with information, not wanting to remember Sam's phone number. She tried to crowd her brain with trivial wonderings: Was there going to be enough time for her to stop at the market tonight? They were out of watermelon, and this time of year she lived on fresh fruit. And Lydia. Her daughter had an audition for a commercial on Monday. Ellen had to remember to look at that big street map of the city that Bob had on the wall of his home office to pinpoint the location of the casting agency holding the audition.

No, there was definitely no room in her head for remembering any numbers. Even ones in an easy sequence like 555–2356.

Ellen wasn't going to call him.

Sam knew that as well as he knew the sun was going to rise in the morning.

She hadn't told him her last name, but he'd heard her paged. Layne. Ellen Layne with a Y. That was a step in the right direction. But still, knowing her full name wouldn't help him find her local phone number. She was staying in town for only a few months. Wherever she was staying, the phone probably wouldn't be in her name.

She wasn't going to call him, and he couldn't call her. And it was a damned shame, because he'd honestly liked Ellen Layne.

Sometimes he had short-term relationships with women he didn't have more in common with than a healthy case of mutual attraction. But as he was talking to Ellen, he'd found himself looking forward to seeing her again, to going out with her, to learning more about her.

She was the first woman he'd ever met who had actually admitted she didn't like art museums.

Yeah, he liked her. A lot.

Of course, the fact that she was a total babe didn't hurt.

She had thick, shoulder-length strawberry blond hair. And her eyes . . . She had the kind of dark brown eyes that seemed as if they were giant, bottomless pits to fall into.

And that body underneath those prim clothes . . . She was slender and trim with soft curves in all of the right places. Her clothing was nice too. Quality.

In fact, everything about her was quality.

She was classy.

But that wasn't why Sam was drawn to

her. His attraction to Ellen Layne was more than his usual case of Uptown Girl Syndrome — probably because after he'd had a chance to talk to her, it was clear that she wasn't a girl, *and* she wasn't actually from the wealthy part of Manhattan, despite the fact that she looked the type. Although, if T.S. were here, no doubt he'd be prepared to argue that Connecticut was, in fact, simply an extension of the Upper East Side.

But T.S. wasn't here. Actually, it was *because* T.S. wasn't at the airport right now that Sam was here instead.

T.S. had called Sam this morning in a panic. The writer had agreed to wine and dine an elderly relative of Bob Osborne's tonight — forgetting that this evening was also his three-year-old daughter's first ballet recital.

From what Sam could gather, T.S. was in the middle of negotiations with the famous talk show host. T.S. wanted to write Bob Osborne's authorized biography, covering everything from his well-to-do childhood to his three-year stint in Vietnam to his battle with substance abuse and all the way up to his recent rise in popularity on network television. Bob had called T.S., asking him to have dinner with his aunt, and in return, he said he'd go ahead and give his approval for the book.

T.S. had tried to call Bob back to explain about his must-attend prior commitment, but the talk show host was unavailable, unreachable — totally out of touch.

That was when T.S. had called Detective Sam Schaefer of the New York City Police Department.

They'd been best friends since fifth grade, and Sam was more than willing to help out his buddy.

He hadn't thought it was important to tell T.S. that tonight was his first night off-duty in close to three weeks. He didn't mention that he and his partner had been working a case that had given him a mountain of overtime hours and little time to relax. Or socialize. In any way.

It was just bad luck that he had been between relationships these past few weeks. Of course, he spent most of his time between relationships, since none of his relationships ever lasted more than a week or two. Some were even shorter.

But Sam had learned through experience that starting a relationship took more time and energy than continuing or ending one. And he hadn't had time to start a new one while working overtime. This particular in-between-relationships period had been dragging on for months now.

But now that his case was over, he'd been toying with the idea of "coincidentally" bumping into the precinct's pretty new administrative assistant as she was leaving work. He had been thinking about inviting her out for drinks and, if that went well, dinner. And if *that* went well, the possibilities were endless.

The truth was, he could have done that last night. In fact, the girl had lingered for a moment at his desk on her way out the door. But Sam had chosen to spend the time finishing up the last of his paperwork.

He'd looked up at the girl, and in a split second he'd played out the time they'd spend together right to the very end.

And it ended ugly.

It ended with tension in the office, with angry words and recriminations, with tears near the water cooler and dark looks in his direction from the precinct captain.

In the past he might have been desperate enough to endure all that for the sake of hot sex with a pretty girl. But these days, knowing that the relationship was going to end badly was the psychological equivalent of throwing a bucket of ice water on his desire.

And it was powerful ice water. He'd been

celibate for many months now, and yesterday, when he hadn't asked the AA out, he'd felt convinced that he could easily handle many more months without sex.

And then Ellen Layne had walked into the airport newsstand. And he'd been just as convinced that he wouldn't last another day without getting it on with this incredible woman. He'd had a solid case of lust at first sight.

Thinking back on their conversation, Sam knew without a doubt that he'd never truly had a chance with Ellen. She'd flirted with him, sure. But that's all it was. An insignificant flirtation.

She'd probably already forgotten his name — let alone his phone number. She'd never call him. Why should she? He was just some potential psycho killer she'd met at the airport.

He'd probably never see her again.

Allowing himself a moment to feel totally depressed, Sam rested his forehead against the glass window, watching Alma's jet maneuver into place near the gate. He wasn't sure why he felt so bad. He met beautiful, vibrant, sexy women all the time. So what if Ellen Layne was more beautiful, vibrant, and sexy than most? She was also — as far as he could tell — a little bit older

24

than most of the women he usually went out with. And from his experience, older women were far more often interested in commitment. And in the past, even just a hint of the C-word was enough to send him running for the hills.

He should be glad she'd walked away. Anything he started with her — even just a single night — had the potential to be incredibly messy and complicated.

But unlike the AA, Ellen Layne didn't work in his office. He could easily walk away from the ugly end of their relationship, couldn't he?

He scoffed at himself. What relationship? The lady clearly wasn't interested.

And that was a shame, because he'd *really* liked her . . .

"Hello, Sam. Don't tell me you're waiting for this flight too?" The voice was unmistakable.

Startled, Sam jerked his head up so quickly, he smacked his nose against the window.

It was her. It was Ellen Layne.

He cared more about not looking foolish than he cared about the spears of pain that were shooting through him. He tried to straighten up in what he hoped was a nonchalant manner as he turned toward

Ellen, hoping she hadn't noticed that he'd damn near broken his nose again.

Her brown eyes were brimming with amusement and concern. "Are you all right? I didn't mean to startle you. Your poor nose."

So much for her not noticing. "I broke it about two months ago," he admitted, letting himself wince as he gingerly touched his face. "I think it's just really sensitive."

"I'm sorry."

He started to open his mouth, but he didn't even get a chance to speak before she cut him off.

"I'm not going to make it up to you by giving you my phone number, so don't even ask."

"Why don't you give me your post office box number," Sam said, "and I'll go in for a psychological evaluation and have the doctor send you a copy of the report. Will that be proof enough for you that I'm not some deranged killer?"

She laughed. She had a low, husky, musical laugh that stirred his blood. "I've heard of people asking other people for blood tests, but sanity tests?"

"Hey, this is New York City. Get used to everything and anything, babe."

The airline passengers were starting to

disembark. Any minute now Ellen was going to meet whomever she was waiting for. And then this time she *would* vanish from his life permanently.

"You know, I've lambasted men for calling me that," she remarked matter-of-factly.

"What? *Babe?*"

"Mmm-hmm."

"Lambasted, huh? Sounds incredibly erotic."

Ellen smiled sweetly. "Oh, trust me, it's not." She stood on her toes, trying to get a look at the people getting off the plane.

He had to do something. And fast. "I swear to God I'm harmless, Ellen," Sam said, talking quickly. "In fact, I'm a cop — a police detective." He took out his badge and handed it to her. "I'd show you my gun, too, but I'm off-duty, so I'm not carrying right now."

He'd managed to surprise her. He took that as a good sign.

"A cop?" She took his badge and looked at it more closely, lightly running her finger over the gleaming gold. "This thing looks real."

"It *is* real. I'm telling you, I'm one of the good guys." God, what was wrong with him? He was standing there with his heart in his throat, praying that she would believe him, praying that she would . . . what? Go home with him? That wasn't going to happen. She was waiting for someone, and *he* was waiting for someone, and . . .

Sam saw Alma. She was wearing a bright red raincoat — exactly as T.S. had described her. Except, wait a minute. There was no way this woman was nearly ninety years old, was there? She *was* about five feet tall, the way T.S. had said, and she *was* wearing a navy blue sweat suit under her raincoat, the way T.S. had said, but this woman couldn't have been a day over seventy, if that.

Still, the woman in the raincoat was looking around as if uncertain as to who exactly was meeting her.

"Excuse me," Sam said to Ellen, sidling his way through the crowd to approach the older woman. Ellen was still holding his police badge, so he had to believe that she wouldn't just disappear on him. At least, he hoped she wouldn't. "Are you Alma?" he asked the woman in the red raincoat.

"Yes, I am," she said, giving him a broad smile. "And that must make you T.S. Harrison, my *favorite* author. Zounds, am I thrilled to meet you!"

"Alma? It *is* you."

Sam turned in surprise to see Ellen enfold the diminutive older woman in an embrace.

"Ellen! Bobby told me you had some sort of acting class," Alma exclaimed. "What a surprise to see you here!"

"I have an even bigger surprise for you," Ellen said, her brown eyes sparkling as she smiled at the elderly woman.

Sam couldn't hold it in any longer. "*You're* here to meet Alma? *I'm* here to meet Alma." He turned to Alma. "And you can't be Alma — Alma's eighty-nine years old. You're too young."

"Fiddlesticks," Alma was saying to Ellen. "What could be a bigger surprise than having dinner with my favorite author?" She smiled at Sam. "Thanks for the compliment, young man, but I'm definitely Alma Osborne. And you can check my driver's license for my age if you want."

"She's going to be ninety next May," Ellen told him. "Longevity runs in the family."

"You've gone blond," Alma said to Ellen. "Let me look at you."

"Something came over me last winter," Ellen admitted, "and I decided to start the new year as a blonde — in hopes of having more fun."

"I like it," Alma proclaimed. "It works for me."

"Works for me too," Sam murmured.

"Did you two come together to meet my

plane?" Alma asked.

There was confusion in Ellen's dark eyes. "*You're* here to meet Alma too?" she said to Sam.

"Do you know who this is?" Alma asked her, pointing at Sam.

"His name's Sam." Ellen glanced down at the police badge she still held in her hands. "Detective Samuel Schaefer." She handed it back to him. "Right?"

"Maybe Sam Schaefer is his given name," Alma told her, "but his pen name is T.S. Harrison. Bobby told me he'd made arrangements for T.S. Harrison to meet my plane, and here he is."

Two

"Um," said Sam, hesitating as he tried to figure out the best way to explain without too badly disappointing the elderly woman.

"*You're* T.S. Harrison?" Ellen was looking at him as if she'd been suddenly struck by lightning. She was clearly impressed. "Why didn't you tell me?"

Now, this was definitely tricky. While Sam enjoyed the wonder and respect that he could see in Ellen's eyes, the last thing he wanted to do was pretend he was something or someone he was not. And as close as they were, he was *not* T.S.

"Well, if you want to know the truth," he started, but was quickly drowned out.

"Alma!" Bob Osborne, surrounded by a team of bodyguards, swept down upon them. "Look at you! You look gorgeous, you old thing, you. How the *hell* are you?"

"Bobby! You're supposed to be in Boston!"

"This is your surprise." Ellen was beam-

31

ing at Alma as Bob swept the tiny woman into his arms and gave her a solid kiss on the cheek.

"Excuse me, but I'm not T.S. Harrison," Sam said, but no one paid any attention at all.

"Harrison! How are you, pal?" One arm still around Alma, Bob turned to shake Sam's hand. "Good to finally meet you in person. All those phone calls. We've been talking, what, for two months? It's a pleasure to be able to look you in the eye."

"Actually," Sam said, "T.S. couldn't —"

But Bob wasn't listening. "Have you met my niece, Ellen Layne? She's staying with me for the summer. El, Harrison here is going to be writing my biography. Get used to his face, kiddo. You'll be seeing a lot of him over the next few months."

"I'm sorry for the confusion," Sam started. "But —"

But Bob had already turned back to his aunt. "Alma, old thing! While I was waiting for your plane, I had *the* most incredible idea. See, I just got a call from my staff in Boston — I've got to get up there pronto. I've got a chartered plane ready to go. But — here's my great idea — why don't you come with me? Postpone your trip to London, call your pals and tell 'em you'll be delayed a few days. Tell 'em you're going to Beantown with your favorite nephew."

"My luggage is already on its way to Lon —"

"They sell sweat suits in Boston, don't they?" Bob looked toward Ellen.

"Of course," she said.

"Of course," he repeated. "I'll buy you whatever you need, put you up at the hotel — it's a *nice* hotel. My treat. Room service, everything. I'll pay for your new airline ticket to London too. Come on, Al, don't say no."

"Well, I wanted to have dinner with T.S. Harrison," Alma said slowly, then grinned at the look on Bob's face, "but I'd much rather go to Boston with my favorite nephew. Unless . . ." She turned to Sam. "How about you come along too? You could interview him on your show, Bobby."

"But I'm not —"

"Harrison's got some revisions to deal with," Bob told Alma. "Besides, he doesn't do television interviews — although with a face like that, the camera would love him. Don't you think, El?"

Ellen just smiled.

"He couldn't possibly come to Boston right now," Bob continued. "He was doing

33

me one hell of a favor just by coming here tonight."

Sam gave up trying to explain. How could he explain when Bob wouldn't even let him get a word in edgewise? Instead he smiled, taking his cue from Ellen. Obviously, she'd learned it was hopeless to try to interrupt.

"Take the limo home," Bob commanded Ellen. He turned to Sam. "Do you have a car and driver waiting?"

He wasn't T.S. Harrison, so of course he didn't have a car and driver waiting for him, but there was no use in trying to explain. He just shook his head no.

"Give Harrison a ride, too, would you mind?" Bob asked Ellen.

"Not at all," she murmured.

"See you in about a week. Tell Lyd break a leg tomorrow." Bob turned to Sam. "I'll have my agent call your agent, get the book deal ironed out."

"It was an honor to meet you," Alma told Sam as she gave Ellen a kiss.

And just like that, they were gone.

Compared to the double chaos of Hurricane Bob and Hurricane Alma, the airport gate was now nearly tomblike in its quiet.

Sam looked at Ellen. "Is it my turn to talk yet?"

She laughed. "Bob can be a little overpowering. Come on, let's leave quickly — before they change their minds."

As they walked, Ellen took a cell phone from her handbag and dialed. "Hi, Ron, it's me," she said into the receiver. "Will you please pull the car around to the front entrance?"

This couldn't be happening. Sam was about to get a ride home from the airport with Ellen Layne. It was like some kind of miracle or sign from God.

But he wanted more than just a ride into Manhattan. Maybe if he played his cards right, he could stretch a short ride into an entire evening. Dinner. Neither of them had eaten yet.

"Are you hungry?" he asked, jogging slightly to catch up with her as they headed toward the escalators that would take them to the terminal's main lobby. "Can I talk you into stopping for something to eat?"

She gave him a look. "Not at one of the airport's restaurants, thanks."

Damn, she was pretty. He pulled back slightly for a moment to admire the way the overhead lights made her reddish blond hair seem to gleam. "We could go wherever you want. I bet when you go out to dinner with your uncle, that's not always an option."

"You're right." Her brown eyes sparkled

as she laughed, and Sam felt his stomach flip-flop. It was going to take them at least forty minutes to get into Manhattan from the airport at this time of night — maybe even longer. Worst-case scenario had him sitting cozily next to her in a limo for all of that time.

Best-case scenario had him gazing into her eyes over a four-course dinner that lasted until well after midnight.

"But I'm a little bit tired," she added. "I'm not sure I'm up to fighting the crowds, waiting an hour for a table. It's Friday, and everyone and their twin sister will be trying to eat out."

"Then how about we stop at a deli, get takeout? We could have a picnic in the limo — have the driver take us for a ride around the city while we eat."

She stepped onto the escalator, turning slightly to look at him. "That sounds like fun," she said. "But —"

"But nothing." He moved onto the step directly below hers. It put them exactly eye to eye. "Come on, it barely even qualifies as outrageous behavior." He played his trump card — the magic word, combined with the truth. "Please, Ellen? I'd love to have a chance to talk to you some more."

Ellen shook her head ruefully as she

looked at him. As long as this man was involved, there would be a certain element of outrageousness in any situation. "I really shouldn't."

"Of course you should. Come on, we both need to eat."

She gazed into Sam's eyes, knowing that she should simply turn him down, right here and right now. Not only was he too young, but he was also too famous. He was T.S. Harrison, for crying out loud. He was the twenty-seven-year-old wunderkind who'd had his first book hit the *New York Times* list before he was even out of college. He was going to be writing a book about her uncle. He was going to be working closely with Bob all summer long. He would be visiting the town house at all hours of the day and night. She would see him all the time — whether she wanted to or not.

It was one thing to share a friendly ride home, but dinner would change the entire tone. Dinner — especially an intimate picnic for two in the back of the limo — would add a gossamer-fine layer of romance onto the evening. And once it was there, it couldn't be removed without crumbling and ruining everything it touched.

Dinner would be a major mistake.

Ellen stepped off the escalator. She could

see Bob's limo waiting outside the glass doors. "Oh, good, it's already here."

As she approached, Ron, the driver, quickly slid out from behind the steering wheel and opened the passenger door.

"You're not going to believe who we're driving home tonight," she said to him. "This is T.S. Harrison." She turned to Sam. "Ron's bought all your books — including your most recent hardcover release. Now, *that's* a dedicated fan, don't you think?"

"Pleased to meet you, sir."

"Actually, my name's really Sam Schaefer," Sam said as he shook Ron's hand. "I'm not —"

"T.S. Harrison is a pseudonym," Ellen told the driver as she climbed into the limo.

Sam climbed in after her and Ron closed the door behind him, sealing them into the muted, shaded privacy of the limousine's belly. The limo had two soft bench seats, facing each other. He could have sat across from her, but he didn't. He sat down next to her. Now, why didn't that surprise her?

"You know, there was something I wanted to talk to you about without Bob around," Ellen told Sam. "I know you're going to be writing about Bob, and I know that his experiences in Vietnam are an important part of what makes him the man he is today, but —"

"Ellen, I have to tell you —"

"No, wait, let me finish, please. I was there when he came back from Vietnam. I was only twelve years old, and I didn't know much about it at the time, but Bob suffered post-traumatic stress syndrome, and when I say suffered, I mean *suffered*. I remember days when he just disappeared — my mother was his oldest sister, and he was living with us because no one else wanted him. I would have to search the woods around our house, looking for him, and . . ." She took a deep breath. "It took him a lot of hard work and a long time to deal with everything that he went through, and I just . . . I'm very protective of him when it comes to this, so I guess what I'm trying to say is, don't you dare push him too hard with your questions. In fact, maybe what you should do is just talk to me, ask *me* about what he did in Vietnam. He lived with us for five years, and I learned how to get him to talk to me about it. It was pretty awful, and I'd just as soon he never had to think about any of it ever again."

He was silent, just sitting there looking at her, a bemused smile playing around the edges of his mouth. "Bob's a lucky man to have you on his side," he finally said.

Ellen held his gaze. "He may have been my uncle, but he was also my best friend. It's been a while since we've been close, but . . ." She smiled. "When you get to know him, when you find out the road he's taken to get where he is today, you're really going to be impressed."

Sam smiled too. "Yeah, I'm looking forward to reading the book, but I'm not going to write it. I'm not really T.S. Harrison."

It took Ellen a moment to make sense of his words. "You're not?" If he wasn't T.S. Harrison, then . . . "Who are you?"

"Like it says on the police badge — Sam Schaefer, NYPD." His blue eyes were filled with chagrin. "I told you in the bookstore, T.S. is a friend of mine. My best friend. Bob asked him to pick up Alma, and he agreed before he remembered his kid had a ballet recital. So he called me. I tried to tell both Bob and Alma that I wasn't T.S., but they wouldn't listen."

Ellen had to laugh. "I thought you were just being modest and cute — you know, telling me at the newsstand that you know T.S. Harrison really well, and then, surprise, you *do* know T.S. intimately — in fact, *you're* T.S."

"If I were T.S. Harrison, I would have told

you who I was right away," Sam countered. "I would have used it to get your phone number — you better believe that, ba—" He stopped himself. "I was going to say 'babe,' but I knew if I did, I'd get lambasted."

"Ooh, a fast learner. I like that in a man."

He grinned. "Although being lambasted still sounds incredibly tempting." His eyes narrowed. "Tell me the truth — would you have given your phone number to T.S. Harrison?"

Ellen adjusted the air-conditioning vent away from her face. "T.S. Harrison already has my phone number, because my phone number is Bob's phone number — at least for the next few months."

"You're avoiding my question."

She smiled. "I know."

"Do you forgive me for not being T.S.?"

"Actually, I'm glad you're not T.S." She was relieved that this man, with his quicksilver smile and bedroom eyes, wouldn't be spending hour upon hour in her uncle's house. "But I'd appreciate it if you could tell the real T.S. all that stuff I just said, you know, about Vietnam?"

Sam nodded. "I will. How about if I have him call you directly too?"

"Thank you."

The phone rang; it was Ron calling from the front seat. Ellen put him on the speakerphone.

"Where to, Ms. Layne?"

She glanced at Sam. "Where are you headed?"

"Hopefully to dinner with you."

Ellen looked into Sam's Paul Newman–blue eyes and made herself face the awful truth. Now that she knew he wasn't T.S. Harrison, and now that she knew he was a police detective and not some weirdo who hung around airport newsstands, she had to admit that she truly liked him. He was funny and smart and incredibly attractive. She *wanted* to have dinner with him. She *wanted* to spend an evening with the dazzle of that charisma focused on her. She wanted to be just a little bit wild. She wanted to take this lighthearted flirtation one teeny little baby-step further.

Nothing heavy. Nothing too intense. Just dinner.

She wanted to.

And she was going to.

So what if he was too young. Age was a state of mind, anyway, wasn't it? Look at Alma. Eighty-nine and going strong.

Still looking into Sam's eyes, Ellen raised her voice enough to be picked up by the speakerphone. "Head for the West Side, please, Ron," she said. "We'd like to stop at the Carnegie Deli and pick something up for dinner. And then, if it's all right with you, we'd like the dollar tour of the city."

"It would be my pleasure," Ron said and signed off.

Sam smiled, a sweet, crooked, utterly charming smile. "Thank you."

Ellen felt herself blush as she let herself be thoroughly charmed. "Well, we both do have to eat and . . ."

Sam was looking around the limo as if seeing the luxurious interior for the first time. "Nice car. I don't suppose the TV has cable?"

Ellen picked up the telephone. "Hello, Ron? Sam just made the old 'Does the limo get cable' joke. How many does that make it? Seven thousand, six hundred and fifty-two times in the past three years that you've had this job? Shall we push him out of the car now, or wait until we're going through the tunnel?"

"Very funny." Sam took the phone out of her hand, listened to make sure Ron wasn't really on the other end, and hung it up. Then he just sat there smiling at her.

Now what?

Ellen nervously searched for something,

*any*thing to talk about. "So . . . how did you meet T.S. Harrison?"

"I refused to steal his 1969 Mets World Series autographed baseball."

"You *what?*"

He grinned. "We were both in fifth grade. Angelo Giglione and Marty Keller — they were seventh graders, and everyone was scared to death of them — they told me that they were going to beat the crap out of me unless I finagled an invitation to Toby Harrison's house and stole this baseball he had that all the Mets on the '69 team had signed."

"*Toby* Harrison?"

"Tobias Shavar Harrison. He decided in ninth grade to do the initial thing — it was around the time he grew a foot and a half taller and made the basketball team. But back in fifth grade he was fat Toby H., the weird science nerd."

Ellen tried not to laugh. "I love the way you talk about your best friend."

"It's the truth. T.S. would be the first to admit it."

"So, what happened?"

"So, Marty and Angelo knew Toby was my science partner, and that he'd have to invite me over to his house to get the project done. I think we were building a volcano.

44

Toby was in charge of making diagrams of tectonic plates, and I was in charge of making the volcano — which was easy, since I'd made a model volcano in the fourth grade and it was still out in my garage. We were both in charge of creating the goo that was supposed to ooze down the sides."

Ellen found herself hanging on to Sam's every word, like some teenager struck with puppy love. She tried to convince herself that she was interested in the story he was telling rather than the slightly rough texture of his voice and the way his graceful mouth moved when he spoke. It didn't take much imagination to picture that mouth moving against her lips, her neck, her . . .

She forced herself to look away from him, forced herself to pay attention to his story.

"So he invited me over," Sam continued, "and I went, and we mixed all this horrible looking stuff together in his kitchen, and his mom even helped us figure out what we had to add to vinegar to make the volcano bubble and foam, and we had a pretty good time. He was an okay guy for a nerd, you know? He really knew how to make me laugh."

It was no use. Ellen couldn't keep from gazing at him, this time into his eyes. She found herself looking closer, trying to see if maybe he wore colored contact lenses. Nobody could have eyes that blue, could they?

"After we finished up with the volcano," he told her, "I sort of casually asked to see this incredible baseball that everyone knew he had. He took me up to his bedroom and took it out of its case and let me hold it. It was so cool. All those signatures. It was worth a lot of money — well, you know, not by grown-up standards, but to a kid . . . I asked him where he got it, and he told me his dad gave it to him.

"Now, when Toby said that, I knew he was full of crap, because everyone knew his dad died in Vietnam before he was born. But then he showed me this letter that his dad had written to him, telling him that his mom was going to hold this baseball for him until his tenth birthday. See, his dad knew he might not come back from 'Nam, so he wrote this letter for this kid that he would never meet."

Ellen forgot about the color of Sam's eyes, totally engrossed in the story he was telling.

Sam smiled at her ruefully. "And so I sat there, looking at all those signatures and the mark of the bat where Wayne Garrett had hit the ball into the stands for a home run. And I looked at the letter, and I looked at

Toby, and I looked at the way he put that baseball back in its special case, and I *knew* that Angelo Giglione and Marty Keller were just going to have to beat the hell out of me, because there was no way I was going to take that baseball away from this kid. And there was no way I was going to let anyone else take it away, either. I told Toby everything, told him to lock that baseball up and not to trust anyone."

Ellen had to ask. "Did they? Those boys? Did they beat you up?"

Sam leaned forward slightly, pointing to a spot on his face just above and off to the side of his right eyebrow. "See this scar? Seven stitches at City Hospital courtesy of Angelo Giglione."

Ellen had noticed that scar earlier. It wasn't a very big scar, yet it managed to add character to his face. It added even more now that she knew where he'd gotten it.

"T.S. only had to get five stitches that day."

"They beat him up too?"

"He saw them corner me on the playground after school, and tried to even up the odds. We've been tight ever since."

She resisted the urge to reach out and lightly trace his scar with her finger. She sat

47

back in her seat, putting some distance between them, suddenly aware that for several long moments his face had been mere inches from hers, his mouth well within kissing range.

She wanted to kiss this man.

It was such a strange sensation. She couldn't remember the last time she'd allowed herself even to think such a thought.

He was looking at her as if he could read her mind. God help her if he could.

But instead of leaning toward her and covering her mouth with his, Sam turned and opened the little refrigerator that was built into the side of the car. "Hey. Look at this. There're five bottles of champagne in here."

"Bob's always ready for anything," Ellen told him as he took one out and looked at the label. She tried to slow the pounding of her heart. "Emmy nominations. High ratings. Viewer's choice awards. Academy Award–winning actresses who might need to be personally escorted back to their hotel after his show . . . Although, you know, he doesn't drink himself."

"I'd heard, yeah." He eyed the glasses and corkscrew that were secured in a nearby compartment. "Do you think he'd mind if we opened a bottle?"

48

"What are we celebrating?"

"Now, there's a myth." Sam unwrapped the plastic from the top of the bottle, exposing the cork. "Who says we need to celebrate something in order to enjoy a glass of champagne? It's really just beer made from grapes."

The phone rang, and again Ellen put on the speaker. "Hang on, folks," Ron's voice said. "I've got a lot of brake lights ahead."

The limo slowed, all the way to a stop.

As Sam watched, Ellen reached for a button on a control panel, and the opaque privacy panel that separated the back of the limo from the front seat went down. She moved across onto the other seat, sitting sideways so that she could look out the front windshield.

"What's going on?" she asked the driver.

He shook his head. "I don't know. But it looks as if some people up ahead are getting out of their cars."

Sam looked at his watch. "There'll be a traffic report on WINS in just a minute."

Ron nodded. "I've been going back and forth between the stations — nobody's said anything about this. I'll let you know as soon as I hear anything. But from the way this looks, we could be here for a while."

Ellen turned back to look at Sam as she

put the panel back into place. "If there's one thing I hate about New York City, it's the relentless traffic. I hope you don't need to be anywhere soon."

"No, I've got the whole night." For the first time in his life, Sam was ecstatic about being stuck in a traffic jam.

Who said they had nothing to celebrate?

He smiled and popped the champagne's cork.

THREE

"My all-time favorite movie?" Ellen mused, leaning back against the soft leather of the seat, her sandals off and her feet up on the facing seat. "That's a hard one. I think it's a toss-up between *E.T., The Sound of Music,* and *The Usual Suspects.*"

Sam laughed as he poured himself another glass of champagne. "I can see your problem deciding," he teased. "They're all so similar."

His feet were up on the seat, too, and Ellen nudged his foot with her toe. "They *are.* They're all great movies."

Sam shifted slightly, moving closer to her so that their feet were touching all the time. "More?" he asked, holding out the bottle.

Ellen shook her head. "No, thanks. At least not until we can get something to eat to go with it." She looked down at their feet — his were still touching hers — and then up into his eyes.

"So, tell me what made you decide to come to New York City for the summer," he said with a smile.

Ellen had to laugh. "This is my fault, isn't it?" she asked. "I touched you first, so now you figure it's okay to touch me."

He still didn't move his feet away. He'd pulled off his white athletic socks when he'd taken off his sneakers, and his feet were warm, with straight, evenly shaped toes. But compared to his arms and hands, his feet were lily white, as if he didn't spend much time with his socks and sneakers off. They were nice to look at, though, and even nicer to feel against her own slightly chilly toes.

He took another sip of his champagne as he gazed at her. "I'd rather hold your hand, but I thought I'd start slowly. You have to admit I've shown incredible restraint, considering we've been sitting here together for . . ." He glanced at his watch. "Nearly two hours."

"Your subtlety has been astonishing," Ellen agreed, "for a man who claims not to be subtle."

He reached across her to set his wineglass in an inset holder along the side of the interior, and their shoulders touched. But when he shifted back, he didn't move far enough away. She wasn't all that surprised when he picked up her hand and laced their fingers together.

The sensation made her heart accelerate, but she couldn't seem to pull away. She didn't *want* to pull away.

"You seem just a little gun-shy," he told her softly, bringing her hand up to his lips. "I'm trying really hard not to scare you."

"I'm not scared," Ellen said. And she wasn't. She knew with a certainty that all she had to do was not move, and Sam would kiss her. All she had to do was to sit right there and just look at him, and he would lean over and . . .

But he didn't.

He just smiled at her, a slow, steady heat burning in his eyes.

They'd been talking nonstop for nearly two hours as they sat in stopped traffic on the Van Wyck Expressway. Ron had relayed news reports that said a tractor-trailer had jackknifed on the road ahead of them, nearly crushing three cars. Apparently there were three different teams with three different Jaws of Life working to free seriously injured passengers. A bevy of choppers had landed on the highway, too, waiting to airlift the injured to the hospital. The road would be blocked for another hour or so.

There was nothing they could do but wait.

And talk.

And open a second bottle of Bob's expensive champagne.

Ellen had told Sam a little bit — just a little bit — about her twelve-year farce of a marriage to Richard. He'd told her a little bit about his childhood in Brooklyn — growing up the son of a second-generation New York City cop, and the pressure he'd felt as the eldest son to follow in his father's and grandfather's footsteps and join the police force. They'd talked about books and movies. They'd touched on the latest fashion trends and argued about the future of pop music. They'd talked about the best place to get Chinese food in the city, and the best place in the Village to get a Middle Eastern meal.

She hadn't told him about her children. As dearly as she loved Lydia and Jamie, she wanted — for just one night — to feel young and wild. And someone young and wild and on the verge of kissing a man nearly ten years her junior surely didn't have a fifteen-year-old daughter and a thirteen-year-old son.

And he *was* going to kiss her. Ellen realized he was simply taking his time. She liked him even more for that, and she loved the anticipation that seemed to stretch way out with each passing second.

He was gazing at her lips now, and he glanced up into her eyes one last time before he leaned forward and covered her mouth with his own.

He skipped all the rules of a traditional first kiss and swept his tongue possessively into her mouth, as if they'd been lovers for years. He tasted like champagne, sweet and delicious as he kissed her deeply, passionately. She felt herself respond to him completely, fire racing through her veins. Lord, it had been so long . . .

She wanted to wrap her arms around him, but she was still holding her wineglass.

Sam lifted his head long enough to take the glass from her hand and set it down next to his. And then he kissed her again, as if he'd never stopped — as if he never intended to stop again.

His hair was impossibly soft as she ran her fingers through it. His arms and his back were incredibly hard, his muscles taut and firm. But even as her hands explored his body, his hands did the same to her, touching her hair and the bare skin of her arms, sending shivers of desire down her back.

She was in *big* trouble here . . .

"Ellen, I want to make love to you." His

fingers found the edge of her shirt and swept up along her skin, covering the softness of her breast, caressing her, touching her so intimately.

She may not have been scared before, but now she was scared to death — not from the way Sam touched her, but from the way his touch made her feel.

Ellen wanted to make love to him too.

Desperately.

She pulled away from him, nearly leaping all the way across the limo.

Sam knew he'd gone too far, and he apologized instantly. "I'm sorry," he said. "I shouldn't have pushed. I didn't mean to . . ."

From the other side of the limo, Ellen laughed. It was shaky, but it was a laugh. "If that was the way you kiss when you don't mean to, I'm afraid to have you kiss me when you *do* mean to."

She was gorgeous. With her blouse half untucked from her skirt and her hair disheveled and her mouth slightly swollen from the roughness of his five o'clock shadow, she was breathtakingly sexy. Her pulling away from him that way should have made him start to cool down. Instead he felt himself grow even harder.

She reached for her glass and took a long, bracing swallow. As Sam watched, she licked a drop of wine from her beautiful lips, and about a hundred incredible fantasies flashed crazily through his mind.

None of which were going to happen tonight, he told himself firmly. Yes, he'd kissed her, and yes, she'd kissed him back as if she'd spent the past decade on a desert island without a man. Yes, she'd surprised him and totally turned him on with the intensity of her response. Yes, she'd kissed him in a way he'd never been kissed before, but the reality of the situation was that she wasn't going to sleep with him tonight.

He took a deep breath, and let it out quickly, shifting slightly in his seat. "So, why did you come to New York? Most people go to Connecticut for the summer to escape the heat."

The telephone rang, and Sam laughed. "I'm destined to never hear the answer to that question." He reached to switch on the speakerphone as he'd seen her do earlier.

"Heard another traffic report," Ron announced. "They got that little girl out of that car, and the last of the choppers left for the hospital. They're going to start working now to clear the road. Should be no more than another ten minutes before we start moving."

"Thanks, Ron," Ellen said.

Sam switched off the phone. "Maybe we should call the deli and order so that we don't have to wait — we can just pick up the food."

"You still want to have dinner?"

"Yeah, I'm starving, aren't you?"

Ellen moved back across the limo so that she could reach the phone. It also put her within his reach, but he was careful to stay securely in his corner, hoping that after she made her phone call she'd stay where she was too. And then he could start inching his way in her direction . . .

"Hi, Ron?" she said into the phone. "Are you still up for stopping at Carnegie Deli? You are? Great. We're going to call in our order — what can we get for you?" She paused. "I'm probably going to have a Reuben sandwich. You too? Excellent. We'll call it in." She hung up the phone and quickly dialed another number.

"How long have you been in town?" Sam asked.

She glanced at him. "Four days."

"And you've already memorized the phone number of Carnegie Deli? I'm impressed."

Ellen smiled at him. "I made a vow not to cook all summer long. And since Bob takes his chef with him when he goes out of town, we've — *I've* — been living on takeout —

Hello? Darn, they put me on hold. Ron and I are having a Reuben. What do you want, Sam?"

What do you want, Sam? It was one hell of a loaded question. Her cheeks flushed slightly as he simply gazed at her. He wanted her, and she knew it.

"Just make it three," he finally said. "Get us some potato knishes, too, and a half a pound of cole slaw. Oh, and cheesecake. Definitely cheesecake."

Ellen placed the order, then hung up the phone. Sam willed her not to move, and she didn't.

"I've never done anything like this before," she said. "Take the entire summer off and come to New York City, I mean. I usually teach a summer course or two."

"You're a teacher?"

"College professor. Freshman English."

He moved a little closer. "What colleges are in Connecticut? I can't think of a single one besides the University of Hartford —"

"I teach at Yale," she told him.

"Yale," he repeated. "Yeah, Yale would be in Connecticut, wouldn't it? Yale, huh? As in really smart kids and even smarter professors?"

"It's not that big a deal."

"I think I'm intimidated," he said, inching

toward her.

Ellen laughed. "You? I don't think the word's in your vocabulary."

"Do you have, like, a master's degree or something?"

"A Ph.D."

"So I'm sitting here, about to put the moves on *Doctor* Ellen Layne?"

"Are you intending to put 'the moves' on me again?"

Sam inched closer. "I have a thing for smart women."

Ellen rolled her eyes. "Something tells me you have a thing for women. Period."

"We're not talking about me right now," Sam pointed out as he moved close enough to take her hand. "We're talking about you. So, you blew off your summer teaching gig to come to the city for the summer — obviously not to make the rounds of the art museums."

She had nice hands — fingers that were nearly as long as his but much more slender, with well-manicured nails, and soft, smooth skin. She wore no jewelry, no rings. She wasn't one of those divorced people who clung to the past by refusing to remove her wedding band. That was a good sign.

Ellen gazed down at their hands, at the way he caressed the inside of her wrist with a slow movement of one finger.

"Actually," her voice was slightly breathless, "I came to New York to try my hand at being an actress." She looked up into his eyes and smiled. "In addition to memorizing Carnegie's phone number, I've also gone on five different auditions in the past four days. One of them was for a part in a soap opera." She laughed. "I don't know what I'll do if I actually get the job."

"Move to New York."

"It's not that easy."

"Hey, it sounds like it's been pretty easy so far. Most people come to New York to be an actor and it takes them years just to find an agent to send them on auditions. First week you're here, you're reading for what, *Guiding Light*? *As the World Turns*?"

"Actually, it's a new show in development. How do you know so much about this?"

"An . . . ex-neighbor of mine finally got a part on *ATWT*, only to get killed off a few weeks later — her character, that is. I, um, helped her load her truck when she decided to head for Los Angeles." He didn't quite meet Ellen's eyes, using the fact that the limo was moving as an excuse to look out the window. "Here we go," he said. "Finally."

Ex-neighbor, huh? Ellen somehow

doubted the ex-neighbor, whoever she was, would have described her relationship with Sam in quite those words. Ex-girlfriend, perhaps. Or maybe ex-lover.

But Ellen didn't really want to know. She didn't want to care. In fact, she refused to care. Sam Schaefer was with *her* tonight. She wasn't interested in anything more than right here and right now. The past didn't matter, nor the future. All she had to worry about was this single moment in time, with his fingers caressing her hand, and his eyes caressing her face.

Ellen knew in that moment that she was going to kiss Sam again. Probably more than once. But she was a big girl. She was a full-grown woman. She could tell the difference between reality and fantasy — and what was happening here in this limousine was definitely fantasy. This man was not only far too young for her, but he was clearly not the type who invested in the long term when it came to relationships. It was more than obvious that everything they said and did in this protective bubble inside the limo would dry up and blow away the second they tried to bring it out into the real world.

"So, how'd you get an agent so quickly?"

he asked, once more able to look into her eyes.

"It's usually one of these weird vicious-circle things," she said. "You know, you can't get an agent until you land a job, and you can't get a job until you have an agent?"

Sam nodded. "So I've heard."

"Well, I lucked out last spring. I was in the right place at the right time, and — trumpet fanfare please — I was cast in a national TV commercial. After that, I got to pick my agent. I picked a good one."

"What's the commercial for? Have I seen it?"

Ellen shook her head. "Probably not. It's supposed to start running some time this summer, but I don't think it's out yet. It's one of those awful laundry detergent commercials. I play a mom who's mistaken for her teenage daughter because her clothes are so clean. Or something."

"There's no way you're old enough to have a teenage daughter."

Ellen just smiled.

"So . . . what if you do get this soap opera job? Would you leave Yale?"

She answered him as honestly as she could. "If it were simply a question of what *I* wanted to do, yeah, maybe I would. When I first started out, I loved teaching, but . . ."

She shook her head. "These past few years I've been dragging myself to work. I'm afraid I'm burned out. I feel like I'm wasting my students' time and money. I feel so ineffective and exhausted and why am I telling you this? You don't want to hear this."

Sam squeezed her hand. "Hey, don't try to second-guess what I do or don't want to hear. This is obviously something that's bothering you, and, as a matter of fact, I can relate."

Without his devil-may-care smile, he looked harder, older, and remarkably world-weary.

"To tell you the truth, Ellen, I've been trying to deal with burnout too. It's hard to walk away, though, when the precinct's staffed with too few people who know what the hell's going on and too many people who don't." He laughed, but it was a harsh, brittle sound. "And of course, there's my father. I don't know how the hell to tell him I'm tired of living his dream. And what do I do if I do leave? I've got to weigh all *that* baggage against the fact that I feel like I'm not getting the job done. I've started wondering if maybe I'm a risk to the men and women I'm working with, and . . . It makes for some sleepless nights, if you know what I mean."

"I know *exactly* what you mean," Ellen whispered. "How can I give up my tenure and my position at Yale for a short-term contract as an actress in a soap opera? If the job doesn't work out, then what? I've got bills to pay." College educations to help pay for. Lord, the thought was terrifying. "Yet at the same time, I've got to think about the kids I'm trying to teach. They deserve a teacher who wants to be there with them. I'm hoping this summer in New York will give me what I need. Maybe I don't need a major change in my life." She snorted. "Other than the obvious change I got when I kicked Richard out. I'm hoping I just need a vacation."

"Maybe what you need is a summer romance."

Their gazes locked. Ellen could feel her heart pounding, feel the recent memory of his lips against hers. And then he touched her, lightly trailing his fingers through her hair, along her cheek, down to her chin.

All of his charming, cheerful, lighthearted facade was still stripped away, leaving bare the emotions on his face and the stark heat in his eyes. "Maybe this summer we'll both find what we're looking for," he added quietly.

What awful things had he seen with those

seemingly ancient eyes? Ellen had to wonder what had happened to make this man doubt himself so completely. Or maybe it wasn't any one specific thing. She'd watched her share of police dramas on TV, and she'd turned her head away at the sight of ghastly, awful crimes. But that was just fiction. Sam's life was real. He lived the awfulness and the danger every single day.

He tugged her closer, and she went into his arms, lifting her mouth to his.

Again his lips seemed so familiar, his kiss like coming home. It was the strangest thing. Because for years no one had touched her but Richard.

She'd been scared to become sexually involved again after her divorce. For the past three years, she'd stayed far away from men because she'd been afraid that she wouldn't care for another man's touch. She was frightened she'd regret her decision, terrified she'd be forced to face the fact that she'd left the only man she'd ever wanted. Richard, despite his failures in the fidelity department, had been an extremely accomplished lover.

But she had been wrong — really wrong.

She wanted Sam with a dizziness that made her glad his arms were around her, holding her tightly, keeping her from falling.

His kisses were familiar and at the same time so utterly different, so passionate, so alive. He kissed her fiercely, possessively, with a scarcely contained desperation.

How long had it been since she'd felt needed like this?

There were other differences too. The way he smelled. Like Richard, he wore a cologne, but his was less spicy, more natural. It was lighter, fresher, more elusive. His lips were softer, his beard sharper, his hair silkier, his arms bigger.

Sam was both bigger and smaller than Richard. He was shorter than Richard by at least three inches. But while Richard had been slender, almost willowy, Sam was muscular and powerfully built. His legs were stronger, his chest broader, his shoulders wider, his arms harder, his hands larger. It was a strange sensation to feel those strange arms around her, to feel those strange hands exploring her body, touching her breasts.

Sam pulled back, breathing hard. "We're almost at the deli. But suddenly I'm not so hungry anymore."

Ellen looked into the eyes of this man who wasn't Richard as she extracted herself from his arms. "I'm not either," she admitted, losing herself in the crackling blue fire burning there. She smiled and began putting on her sandals. "But someone's got to buy Ron his sandwich."

FOUR

"Ron still thinks you're T.S. Harrison," Ellen told Sam as she unwrapped one of the Reuben sandwiches. "He told me he used his car phone to call his wife and tell her he was driving you around. He was so excited, I didn't have the heart to tell him the truth."

She was sitting across from him, her sandals once again kicked off, her legs tucked up underneath her. As Sam watched, she took a bite of her sandwich. She held it up and used her tongue to catch some of the Thousand Island dressing spilling out from between the bread.

He was staring. He knew he was staring, but he was mesmerized by her mouth. He couldn't think of anything besides how much he wanted to kiss her again.

That wasn't entirely true. He *could* think of one other thing — the condom he had bought from the vending machine in the deli men's room. It was burning a hole in his pocket.

He wasn't really sure why he'd bought it. Maybe it was the way she'd kissed him right before they arrived at the deli. Maybe it was wishful thinking.

He'd spent most of the past few hours believing that if he was going to get lucky with Ellen Layne, it wasn't going to happen tonight. But then he was standing there in front of that vending machine, and he had a sudden, incredibly sharp, amazingly clear image in his head of Ellen, in his arms, minus most of her clothes, stretched out in the backseat of that limousine. So he bought a condom. God forbid he be caught without one.

He kept an entire box of them in the glove compartment of his car. But his car was all the way across town, in the precinct parking lot, where he'd left it all those hours ago, before he'd gone out to the airport to do a favor for T.S.

It seemed like a lifetime ago. It was before he'd known he would sit in traffic for two hours, trapped in a small space with the most attractive woman he'd met in a good long time.

It was before Ellen.

"Aren't you going to eat?" she asked.

Sam unwrapped his sandwich. It smelled good. As he took a bite he realized he was ravenous. He'd never tasted anything so delicious in his entire life, and he'd eaten at Carnegie Deli plenty of times before.

It was odd — as if all of his senses were heightened.

"So you and T.S. stayed close even after grade school?" Ellen asked in between bites of her sandwich.

Sam nodded. "We both played on the basketball team in high school."

"I think I read somewhere that T.S. went to NYU. Did you go there too?"

"No, I, uh, didn't." What was the big deal? So what if she was a professor at an Ivy League university. So what if he had nothing more than a high school diploma. "I didn't go to college."

Ellen was surprised. "But you seem so . . . I don't know, so well read, I guess."

"I love to read — I always have. But when I was a kid, I loved baseball more than homework, and when it came time to apply for scholarships, my grades weren't worthy of any financial aid. And my old man only had enough money saved to send two of us three kids to college. It would've been me and my brother because we were the oldest, but I knew how badly Joni, my sister, wanted to go. . . ." He shrugged. "The rest is history."

Sam took another bite of his sandwich, aware that she was watching him, her brown eyes searchingly intense, as if she were trying to read his mind.

"What about how badly *you* wanted to go?" she asked quietly.

She *could* read his mind. He shook his head, talking with his mouth full. "I really didn't want to go." He swallowed. "At least not as much as Joni did."

"But what if someone had insisted? Would you have gone if you were given a scholarship?"

He smiled. "Yeah, okay, you're right. I *did* want to go. I just . . . wanted Joni to go more. It was no big deal."

Her eyes were soft and so warm. "You know perfectly well it was a very big deal."

"Yeah, right, I'm a real hero. Let's talk about something else, shall we?" He reached for the open champagne bottle, filled both of their glasses, and handed Ellen's to her.

"Thanks." She took a sip. "You know you could go to night school. It would take you more than four years to get a degree, but —"

"Nah, I never know when I'm going to have to work nights." He took another bite of his sandwich. "Hey, these things are good, aren't they?"

She put her sandwich down, leaning toward him, gesturing with her champagne flute. "You said yourself that you're considering leaving your job. You could go to school full-time. I think you'd really like it — even the homework."

He sighed. "I don't want to, okay? Can we change the subject —"

"How could you not want to —"

"I just don't." He drained his glass.

"Sam, if you don't have the money saved, you could probably —"

"I've got plenty of money saved, I just don't *want* to —"

"You wanted to ten years ago."

"That's right. Ten years ago. Ten *years*." He refilled his glass. "I'm too old, all right? I'd feel silly — I'd be ten years older than everyone else in my class."

"You are so wrong about that. I sometimes have people in my freshman English class who are older than *me*." She was leaning forward so far, she was in danger of falling off the seat. Her brown eyes were blazing, her face aglow with her need to prove him wrong.

Sam met her gaze, wondering if she could see the fire that had just ignited inside of him, wondering if she could feel the air almost crackle around them with electric expectation and desire. "Why don't you come over here and convince me?" he said softly.

To his surprise, she didn't back away. Instead she smiled. She had an incredible smile — a smile that lit her entire face. Sam found himself smiling back at her.

"You really don't like to talk about yourself, do you?" she asked. "You can probably get away with just that smile, am I right? That smile and a couple of distracting kisses, and you don't need to say a single word about the things you really care about or the way you really feel."

Sam couldn't deny it. "So what do you want to know about me? I'm not sure I can put into words what I'm feeling right now, but I could probably manage to show you —"

"Don't get cute. Just . . . tell me about yourself. Talk. Where have you been? What have you done? Did you join the police force right out of high school?"

That was an easy one to answer. "No, I spent two years in the Marines first. A recruiter came to our high school and made it sound as if we'd immediately be sent overseas, you know, stationed in Europe —

cheese, wine, French girls, ooh la la . . . My father was pushing for me to go right into the police academy. I think I figured it was my last chance to do something for myself. I wanted to see Paris and Rome. The Greek Isles." He laughed. "I spent the first year in Kansas, the second in South Dakota. I hated every minute of it, but I was damned if I was going to let the old man know I'd made a mistake." He smiled at her. "How was that? Personal enough for you?"

Ellen smiled back, taking another sip of her wine. "It's a start. Keep going."

"Are you sure it's not time for a few of those distracting kisses?"

She laughed. "Definitely not. Keep going."

"All right. Let's see. I guess I can tell you that in retrospect, my two years as a Marine were a good thing. I made it through basic training — in fact, I got really strong, and that was good. Also, spending a few years away from home was very cool. It may not have been Paris, but the Badlands were incomparable. I made some good friends, learned a lot of Native American history, lived through a tornado or two, and totally pissed off my father in the process, which is every eighteen-year-old's fondest desire. Yeah, it wasn't as bad as I thought."

"Then you came back to New York and

joined the police force?"

"Correct for ten points. I went in, passed all the tests, and became a uniformed cop. I made detective five years ago, and . . . here I am."

"Thinking about quitting."

Sam winced. "We already talked about that. Are you sure you don't want to discuss something easier, like old girlfriends?"

"I think there's probably too many of them to talk about — we'd be here all night."

Again, Sam couldn't deny it. "When do I get to grill you about your old boyfriends?"

Ellen shrugged. "Ask away. I only had one. Adam Webster. He moved away in the middle of senior year. High school. We were in love, I really think we were, but his father got a job in Ohio. We wrote for a while, but . . ." She took a delicate sip of her champagne. "And then there was Richard, whom I married. Foolishly."

Two men. There had only been two other men in Ellen Layne's life. Sam couldn't help but hope he'd be number three.

"Your divorce," he said. "It's pretty recent, huh?"

"In the scheme of things, yeah," she said. "We were married for twelve years. Lord, I blush to think about how stupidly naive I was."

"Sometimes the hardest things to see are the things that are right in front of your face."

"Ain't that the truth."

"What'd he do? Have an affair?"

"I think maybe it's time for one of those distracting kisses," Ellen said.

Sam didn't hesitate. He moved across the car and sat down next to her. She set down her glass and turned toward him.

"You're good at this, aren't you?" she asked.

He just smiled. And kissed her.

She seemed to melt into his arms. Her lips were heartbreakingly soft, her mouth as sweet as wine, and he felt a sharp hunger that made him want to kiss her deeper, harder. He wanted to inhale her, to drink her in. He couldn't hold back.

Each time he'd kissed her, he'd meant to kiss her gently, sweetly. But each time, he'd felt this hungry need that he hadn't been able to ignore. And that need was further fueled by the passion of Ellen's response. It was all he could do not to sink down onto the seat with her soft body underneath his. He knew with a certainty that it wouldn't take much for him to seduce her. A little more wine, a few more kisses, and that condom he'd bought would be put to good use.

He lifted his head. "Richard's a fool. How could anyone cheat on *you?*"

She touched his face, tracing the scar alongside his right eyebrow. "Richard didn't seem to be able *not* to cheat," she told him. "He was so good at it, I probably never would have found out — if he hadn't had to go into the hospital with a burst appendix. You have gorgeous hair."

Sam refused to be distracted by her fingers running through his hair. "Please don't tell me you ran into his mistress at the hospital."

She stopped touching him, pulling back, out of his arms. Sam caught her hand before she moved too far away.

"It was nothing that dramatic," she told him. "Richard was in the hospital for nearly three weeks — there were complications from his surgery, nothing too serious, a slight infection, but they wouldn't release him until it cleared up. While he was there, I realized that all of our bills were really piling up. He had been in charge of writing the checks to pay our bills ever since we were first married, but I figured that would be the last thing he'd want to do after he got out of the hospital, so I thought I'd surprise him and take care of it for him. I was the one who got the surprise — from his credit card bills."

She took a deep breath and let it out in a rush. "There were weekly charges made to a hotel that wasn't more than thirty minutes from our house."

Sam knew exactly what was coming. He wanted to kill the bastard, but all he could do was hold Ellen's hand. So he held it. And he listened.

"I knew right away that I was looking at something Richard wouldn't want me to see — so of course, I looked further. He kept meticulous files, and I was able to go back nearly seven years through his records, and I could see . . ." Her voice wavered, but she cleared her throat and started again, her voice stronger this time. "I could see through his credit card purchases exactly when he'd started each new affair. He would buy her — whoever she was — something from a lingerie catalog. He would buy her a pricey piece of jewelry. There'd be a flood of charges to expensive restaurants for lunches and dinners. And of course, there were those hotel room charges — sometimes two, three, or even four times a week. He wouldn't stay overnight. He'd just use the room at lunchtime or whenever. Maybe right after work." She laughed, but it was a dry, humorless sound. "Then he'd come home to me." She imitated herself: "Hi, honey. You're so late tonight. Tough day at work? Poor baby, let me rub your back for you. . . ." She closed her eyes. "God! What a bastard!"

"Finding out must've hurt so badly," Sam murmured. "It must *still* hurt."

"I feel really stupid," Ellen told him. "How could I not have known? I seriously didn't have a clue. And he'd been doing this for at least seven years. I had the proof in those credit card bills. That pattern of purchases was repeated, over and over, nearly eight times in the past seven years. And I have no reason to believe that if I had access to the years before that, I wouldn't find a similar pattern."

"What did you do?" Sam asked softly.

"First I threw up," she told him with a crooked smile. "And then I packed up his clothes and kicked the son of a bitch out. I got a lot of crap for that — after all, the man was in the hospital at the time. Needless to say, I felt more than a little bit betrayed and didn't give a damn what anyone thought. I filed for divorce that same day." Ellen reached for her champagne glass and took a sip. "You know, I *do* have something to celebrate. Day after tomorrow is the third anniversary of my divorce."

Three years. Sam was surprised it had been that long. Her wounds seemed much more recent.

"I think we should have a toast," Ellen said, filling her glass. "To a summer in New York City. Richard hated New York City. He hated Bob. And you know what? When he sees it, he's going to hate that commercial I made. He's gonna hate that I dyed my hair blond. He would have hated your hair too — and you can take that as a compliment."

Sam ran one hand self-consciously through his hair, still holding her close with the other. "Too long for old Richard?" he asked.

"Too long, too blond, too sexy, too still-on-your-head." Ellen ran her fingers through the hair in question. "Richard is . . . hair challenged. Before the end of the decade, he's going to be nearly entirely bald."

Sam laughed, kissing her, his own hands exploring the softness of her curves, the smooth firmness of her bare thigh. "You sound just a little too happy about that."

"He lied to me for twelve years. If God sees fit to make him lose all of his hair, who am I to complain?"

Sam covered her mouth with his again,

but she pulled away before he could deepen the kiss. "Richard would hate the way I've been kissing you. Such a typical double standard."

"Richard's not here," Sam said, kissing her eyes, her face, her neck.

"Do you know what Richard would *really* hate?" she asked.

This time Sam pulled back. He gazed into the midnight darkness of her eyes, well aware of what she'd intended to imply. Richard would really hate it if they made love. He knew he shouldn't say anything. He knew he should simply kiss her, and keep kissing her until their clothes were pushed aside and he was buried deep inside of her. She wanted him to make love to her — to get back at the man who had hurt her so badly.

What the hell did he care why she wanted him? She wanted him — that should've been enough.

But it wasn't, and he couldn't believe the words that came out of his mouth. "That's not a very good reason for us to be together," he said softly.

She took another fortifying sip of her champagne and closed her eyes. "I know," she murmured. "But it's not the only reason."

Ellen opened her eyes and looked at Sam. His hair was a mess, his tie loosened and askew, the top button of his shirt undone. He looked incredibly handsome with those blue eyes and that perfectly sculpted face, those adorable dimples. He wanted her — she could see it in his eyes — and knowing that gave her the strength to tell him the truth.

"I haven't been with anyone since I left Richard," she said softly. "It's been more than four years, but I haven't wanted to. I haven't wanted any kind of intimacy — not until now."

His eyes sparked at her words. "And how many years has it been since you've helped to kill two bottles of champagne?" he asked, his voice husky.

"I'm not drunk," she told him. Yes, the wine had lowered her inhibitions, but she wasn't drunk. She reached out to touch his face. "You're so sweet — you're trying to protect me from myself, aren't you?"

"I just want to make sure you know what you're doing." He closed his eyes as he pressed his cheek into her palm.

"I know exactly what I'm doing. I've spent my entire life doing things other people expect of me," she countered. "I came to New York this summer to do something for

myself, to do the things that I want to do."
She lowered her voice. "And I think you
know what I want to do right now."

It was all that Sam needed to hear.

Once again Ellen let him take the glass
from her hand and set it down. Then he
kissed her again.

It was one hell of a dizzying kiss, and
somehow, in the course of it, he managed
to pull her gently down onto the seat with
him.

He stopped for a moment to shrug out of
his jacket and to pull off his tie, and then he
kissed her again — long, slow, deep kisses
that nearly made her unable to think.

Nearly.

As Ellen closed her eyes and wrapped her
arms around this man she barely knew, she
vacillated wildly between wondering what
the hell she was doing and being thoroughly
convinced that she was one hundred percent
right.

She *was* right. She was exorcising the
ghosts of her past with this young, handsome, willing stranger. She was the self-
proclaimed queen of sex-only-with-
commitment-and-love — God knows she'd
preached about it enough times to her kids.
But in an attempt to regain control of her
life, she was in the process of having a one-

night stand.

In the back of a moving limousine.

With a man ten years her junior.

Who happened to look like a movie star.

And kiss like an angel from heaven.

Sam shifted slightly, so that he was lying next to her on the soft leather of the seat, one arm around her, one leg pressed between hers, hiking her skirt up. He kissed her again, his tongue taking lazy possession of her mouth, as his free hand gently tugged her blouse from the waist of her skirt. He took his time caressing the softness of her breasts through the silk, took his time unfastening the tiny mother-of-pearl buttons, took his time sliding his mouth down to her chin, her jaw, her throat, her collarbone.

His mouth moved even lower as his fingers unhooked the last button of her blouse, and he kissed her through the soft lace of her bra, touching her with his tongue, pulling, gently at first, then harder.

He unfastened the front clasp of her bra, and Ellen stopped thinking. She could only feel, only shiver, only respond to his hands and his mouth, to his deep inhale of pleasure, to the exquisitely seductive sensation of his skin against hers, to the unmistakable length of his arousal held tightly against her thigh.

She reached between them to unbutton his shirt, needing to feel his skin beneath her hands as well.

Sam pulled back slightly, giving her room, reaching up to help her with the last of the buttons. He would have pulled his shirt off his shoulders and shaken it off his arms, but she stopped him.

"We better keep most of our clothes on," she whispered.

He looked disappointed. "No one can see in these windows."

"I know, I just . . . What if we get into an accident, and —"

He kissed her. "Shhh. It's all right. You don't need to explain. Whatever makes you more comfortable."

He had golden blond hair on his chest and more muscles than she'd ever seen up close and personal. She touched him, lightly at first, then harder. His back was so smooth, the hair on his chest so soft. She could feel his hand, sliding up her leg, pushing her skirt up, nearly to her hips. The sensation was incredible, and she laughed aloud.

"I can't believe I'm doing this."

He smiled at her, a hot, fierce smile. "I can't believe it either. I keep thinking I'm going to wake up any minute."

She reached for his belt buckle. "Do you have a condom? Please say yes."

"Yes." He pulled it out of his pocket and tossed it within easy reach on the carpeted floor.

"Gee whiz, and it's so conveniently handy too." She opened his belt and unfastened the button of his pants. "I must've been shooting out obvious pheromones all evening long. Talk about a sure thing."

"No, I'm just an eternal optimist," he told her with another long, searing kiss. His hands explored the edge of her silk and lace panties, his fingers slipping underneath to find her wet and ready for him. Man, was she ready for him.

Ellen heard herself moan as she lifted her hips toward him, pushing him more deeply inside of her.

Sam nearly lost it. She hadn't even really touched him yet — her fingers were just fumbling gently with his zipper — and he'd nearly slipped over the edge. He couldn't remember the last time he'd been so totally turned on.

It was strange — he would've thought making love this way, with their clothes only unfastened or pushed aside, wouldn't have been as good. But as much as he was dying to see Ellen naked, the sight of her lying beneath him with her beautiful body half hidden by her disheveled clothes was making him crazy. One taut, dark pink nipple peeked out from the silk of her shirt. Her skirt was twisted around her waist, exposing her long, exquisitely shaped legs. He'd all but pushed aside the black silk and lace of her panties and the effect made his blood burn through his veins.

She worked his zipper down, then touched him, covering him with her hand through the cotton of his shorts.

The sensation lit him on fire.

He shifted his weight, pressing himself between her legs, only the fabric of their clothes keeping them from becoming one. Dear God, he'd died and gone to heaven.

Sam kissed her — or she kissed him — he didn't know, it didn't matter. He moved then, stroking her with the length of his arousal, and she moved, too, lifting her hips in rhythm with him.

The promise of ecstasy was too much to take, and Sam moved quickly, pulling himself off of her, slipping her panties down her legs.

She reached for him, trying to push his pants over his hips. He freed himself in one smooth motion, then reached across her for the condom. As his fingers closed around it her fingers closed around him.

"Gotcha," she murmured, and Sam laughed out loud.

She did. She had him. Completely. She owned him. He was thoroughly infatuated. Of course, it was true that he became infatuated with a beautiful woman as quickly and as easily as most people bought a new pair of sneakers, but this was stronger than what he'd felt most of the time. He was willing to bet this crush he had would last for the entire summer. It was also true that a whole summer was about two months longer than his usual romantic fling, but Ellen wasn't usual, in any way, shape, or form.

Sam had a feeling that this was going to be the best summer of his entire life.

He tore open the condom and she helped him cover himself. Actually, her help was debatable — she made both it and him harder, but Sam didn't mind. He was in no hurry. He had the entire summer.

She surprised him by straddling him, by kissing him hungrily as she impaled herself upon him, surrounding him with her tight heat.

There was no doubt about it, he was the luckiest son of a bitch on the planet. She began to move, and he moved with her, gazing into her eyes as she held on to the seat back behind him.

She closed her eyes and her head went back as he shifted his hips, pushing himself more deeply inside of her. This was good. It was *too* good. There had to be some kind of catch.

Whatever it was, it was going to be well worth it for all he was feeling right now.

They were moving slowly, languorously, each thrust of his hips bringing dizzying, melting pleasure. But then the car jerked to a stop, and he reached for her, holding her tightly to keep them both from sliding onto the floor. His movement pushed him up inside of her, sharp and fast and heart-stoppingly deep. They both cried out, and Sam knew that she was as close to release as he was.

And then the phone rang.

They both froze. Ellen opened her eyes and stared directly at him. Then she put one finger to her lips, reached behind him, and pushed on the speakerphone.

"Yes, Ron?" she asked, her voice sounding remarkably normal.

"Everything okay back there?" Ron asked. "Sorry about stopping short like that."

Sam wanted desperately to laugh, and he

could see that Ellen did too. In fact, he realized that she could no longer speak. She buried her face in his neck.

"Not a problem, Ron." He raised his voice to be picked up by the speakerphone. He looked out the window, trying to figure out where they were. "Hey, would you mind taking us past the public library?" That was way on the other side of town. "Ellen hasn't had a chance to see the lions yet."

"Sure thing, Mr. Harrison," Ron said cheerfully.

As Ellen reached up and cut the connection, they both dissolved into laughter.

"I haven't had a chance to see the lions," Ellen repeated. "It sounds like some incredible euphemism. You know, like, 'Was it good for you, honey? Did you . . . see the lions?' "

Sam laughed even harder. God, he couldn't remember the last time he'd been this . . . happy. He caught Ellen's face with both hands, kissing her hard on the mouth. "I'm having more fun tonight than I've ever had in my entire life," he told her.

"I bet you say that to all the women who seduce you in the back of their uncle's limousine."

"Yeah," he agreed. "All one of them."

Ellen felt herself melt as she gazed into

Sam's eyes. There was a softness there, a tenderness that made her feel warm inside. Cared for. Cherished.

He kissed her gently. "I'm serious, Ellen," he whispered. "I swear, I've never felt anything like this before." He kissed her again. Harder this time. Deeper. Longer. And their passion reignited instantly, scorching her to her very soul.

She knew his sweet words were just that — sweet words. Still, she knew it wouldn't take much for her to fall in love with this sexy, gorgeous man.

But what a mistake *that* would be.

She closed her eyes, banishing all thought as she began to move, both with him and against him. Thinking was not allowed. Only feeling. And oh, the way he was making her feel.

He moved faster now, faster and harder and deeper, and Ellen matched his rhythm, losing herself in his kisses and caresses, letting herself spin out of control.

There was no past, no future. There was only this moment, and it was a very, *very* good moment, exploding with light and color and wave upon wave of wild sensation.

Her entire body seemed to shake with the strength of her release, and she felt Sam's body answer. He pulled her mouth down to his for a deliciously ferocious kiss that muffled his groans of pleasure.

Still breathing hard, Ellen clung to him, refusing to acknowledge any of the questions that were trying to break into the aftermath of their passion.

What happens now? Try as she might, that was one question that she couldn't easily ignore.

Ellen peeked out from underneath her eyelashes. Sam's head was back, his own eyes closed.

Without opening his eyes, he smiled slightly and pulled her even closer, holding her tightly but so gently, his hands moving soothingly up and down her back. He sighed with the deepest contentment.

Ellen watched him breathe. His nostrils flared slightly with each breath he took. He had remarkably handsome nostrils. In fact, his nose — and his entire profile — was worthy of an epic poem.

She'd noticed that the first time she'd glanced at him. In the airport newsstand. Only a few short hours ago.

Dear God, what had she done? She'd just made love to a stranger. Ellen felt a rush of tears fill her eyes, and she turned her head away, resting her cheek against his shoulder.

She'd used this man as completely as he'd used her, but her use went beyond mere sexual gratification. She'd used Sam to try to rid herself of Richard, once and for all.

Richard. Lord. She hadn't thought of him, not even once, while she and Sam had been making love. After the differentness of Sam's kisses, she had been so certain she would compare every touch, every caress, every sensation.

But Sam had succeeded in focusing her attention securely on *him,* keeping her thoughts far from Richard.

Richard who? she thought, smiling as she blinked away her tears.

She opened her eyes and found herself looking directly at the steps that led to the public library. She tilted her head slightly, and there they were. Lit from the streetlights. The stone lions.

Ellen snorted with laughter, and Sam lifted his head. "What?" he asked.

"Look."

He leaned over and saw the lions.

What were they going to do next? Ellen knew precisely. They were going to laugh. Giddily. Breathlessly. Deliriously.

She pushed herself up and off of him as he began to laugh too. She laughed as she straightened her skirt and he cleaned himself up, efficiently, expertly, and zipped up his pants. She fastened her bra and buttoned her shirt, tucking it in, still laughing.

"Well, that was just about perfect timing," she said, wriggling back into her panties.

She would have sat across from him, but he reached out and took her hand and pulled her down close to him, his arm around her shoulders. He tugged her chin toward him and covered her mouth with his in a deliciously sweet kiss.

When he pulled back, he searched her face rather intently. "You okay?" he asked softly.

Ellen couldn't quite meet his eyes. "I've never even remotely done anything like this before," she admitted.

"I assumed as much," Sam told her, "considering I'm only boyfriend number three."

She glanced at him. "I'm not sure one night, in the back of a limo, makes you eligible for the title of boyfriend."

"How about two nights in a row, dinner at a real restaurant this time before we go to my place — or yours — and make love in a real bed?"

Ellen shook her head. "I'm not sure that's such a good idea. I think I need some time to recover."

For a brief moment he looked as if he

were about to argue, but then he nodded. "Fair enough."

She was definitely twisted — she absolutely didn't want him to argue with her, but at the same time, she couldn't help feeling a little bit hurt that he hadn't even tried to change her mind.

She looked at her watch. "Wow. I had no idea it was so late."

Sam could recognize a hint when he heard one. Despite the fact that he wanted nothing more than to ride around with Ellen in his arms until the sun came up, he knew that she was ready for him to go. He'd dropped many a similar hint himself in the past — *Would you look at the time? I really should go. . . .*

That didn't necessarily mean anything bad, he tried to reassure himself. It *was* late. Ellen was no doubt also thinking of the driver, who'd been in the limo as long as they had, but who had been having a whole hell of a lot less fun.

He pulled her close to him again and kissed her, his confidence restored at her immediate response. Despite the fact that she didn't want to have dinner tomorrow night, he had to believe from the way she was kissing him that she would definitely want to see him again. Who was he kidding?

Of course she'd want to see him again. Women almost always did.

He wasn't conceited — he was simply able to acknowledge the truth. There were many things he wasn't particularly good at, but seducing a woman — charming her and giving her pleasure throughout an entire evening — now, *that* was one of his strengths.

Sam sat forward slightly, looking out the window, catching the numbers of the cross streets as they went past. "We're not far from my place." They were even closer to where his car was parked in the precinct lot, but he'd had quite a bit of that champagne and he didn't want to drive. Besides, he didn't really want to go, and this would add another three minutes to this incredible, outrageously wonderful evening.

Ellen picked up the phone, buzzing the driver. "Hi, Ron," she said. "We're going to drop Sam off now."

Except Ron would know the instant he pulled in front of Sam's building that Sam wasn't T.S. Harrison. Someone who pulled in a seven-figure advance the way T.S. did wouldn't live where Sam lived. It didn't seem fair to burst Ron's bubble before being able to introduce him to the real T.S. Harrison. That would happen soon enough, but definitely not tonight.

Sam gave Ellen a much more upscale address a few blocks away from his place, and she relayed the information to Ron. The evening was warm and dry; Sam wouldn't mind the walk.

They arrived there much too quickly, and he slipped on his jacket and sneakers, straightening his hair one last time as Ron opened the door for him.

"Ellen," he started, but she touched his lips with one finger.

"You don't have to say anything," she told him, leaning forward to kiss him good-bye.

"Yes, I do," he countered. "Because I still don't have your phone number."

Something flickered in her eyes. "If you really want my phone number, you can probably figure out how to get it."

Sam laughed. "Are you serious? You're not going to give it to me?"

She glanced away from him. "I don't want you to feel obligated to call me."

She didn't think he was serious about wanting to see her again. Well, she was wrong. He was going to get her phone number from T.S. and call her.

But first he was going to give her the time and space she'd asked for.

If what she'd told him was true, he was

the first man she'd let into her life after what had to have been a devastating end to her twelve-year marriage. He couldn't relate — he'd never even had a twelve-*week* relationship — but he *could* understand how she might want a little time to sort her feelings out.

And he had plenty of time. She was going to be in town for the entire summer.

He kissed her again — a long, lingering kiss designed to keep her thinking about him in the days to come.

"Thanks for having dinner with me," he said softly, pulling away, intending to climb out of the car.

But it wasn't going to be that easy. He couldn't keep himself from kissing her again as he felt the unmistakable tug of desire. He wanted her again. Already. It was not a surprise. She looked incredible, sitting there with her hair slightly mussed, the top buttons of her shirt undone just a little too far, a soft, dreamy, sleepy satisfaction in her gorgeous brown eyes. He wanted to wake up with her next to him in his bed.

"You better go," she whispered, her fingers in his hair.

"I know." Sam had to bite his tongue to keep himself from begging her to have dinner with him tomorrow night.

He backed out of the limo, holding her hand until the last possible second.

Ron was standing patiently near the car door, and he closed it, nodding to Sam. "Good night, sir."

Sam extracted some money from his wallet. Ron had been driving all night, and he definitely deserved a hefty tip.

"Good night, Ron, and thanks," he said, pressing the bills into the driver's hand as the two men shook.

Ron glanced at the money. "Oh, no, sir, I couldn't . . ."

"Yes, you could," Sam insisted.

"Thank you, Mr. Harrison."

As the driver climbed behind the steering wheel, Sam gazed at the limo's window, knowing that even though he couldn't see her through the privacy glass, Ellen could see him. And when Ron started the engine, the window slid down.

Ellen's dancing brown eyes and sparkling smile seemed to light up the night. "Good night, Sam," she called to him as the limo pulled away. "I loved seeing the lions."

Sam laughed aloud as he watched the taillights of the limo disappear.

To hell with space and time. He was calling her tomorrow.

FIVE

"Mom! Telephone!" Ellen's thirteen-year-old son, Jamie, came sliding into her bedroom, skidding across the highly polished wood floor in his socks, posing like a surfer, holding out the cordless phone.

She took the phone from him, covering the mouthpiece with her hand. "Who is it?"

"Some guy wid a New Yawk accent," Jamie imitated with comic perfection.

Sam didn't have *that* much of an accent. But, she reminded herself, she wasn't expecting him to call. She didn't *want* him to call. "Hello?" she said.

It wasn't Sam. It was Lydia's agent, calling with information about a second audition for Monday afternoon. Ellen wrote it all down in an appointment notebook she kept on her desk next to her laptop computer, as Jamie attempted clumsily humorous figure-skating moves, still sliding with his socks in the center of the room.

101

"Audition?" he asked as she hung up the phone.

"Yep."

"Who's it for?"

"Lyd." Between the three of them, they'd been kept pretty busy, going from one audition to the next. Both of Ellen's kids had been acting and modeling since Lydia had pointed to the kids on *Sesame Street* and said that she wanted to do that. Jamie had tagged along to several of her early modeling sessions and had signed on soon after.

Since they'd been in New York full-time, there had been more opportunities. They'd gone on every one of what Ellen called "long-shot" auditions, cattle calls, for which they would not have made the drive down from Connecticut. But since they were in the city, they went.

"Not me?" Jamie asked, clearly disappointed. "Are you sure I can't read for the part anyway?"

"You tell me," Ellen said, lifting her eyebrow to look at her son. "Can you play a fifteen-year-old girl?"

Jamie pretended to consider it. He probably hadn't showered yet this morning, and his light brown hair stood up straight, reminiscent of Bart Simpson's. His round wire-rimmed glasses were crooked, as usual, perched atop his freckled nose. His eyes were a beautiful shade of blue-green, rimmed by lashes nearly twice as long as his older sister's — didn't it figure? He had just turned thirteen this past May, but he was small for his age and still auditioning for nine-and ten-year-old roles. Nine-and ten-year-old *boys*' roles.

"I'm an actor," he said with exaggerated gestures, "but even for me, a fifteen-year-old girl would be a stretch. Besides, I'm probably too short," he added à la Groucho Marx, sliding back out of the room.

"Do you know where Lydia is?" Ellen called after him.

"Up in the ballroom, practicing her saxophone," he called back.

Up in the ballroom. Jamie wasn't kidding. Bob's town house was like something out of an old movie starring Katharine Hepburn and Cary Grant. The house — if you could call it a house and not a palace — was five stories high, with both an elevator and a sweeping marble staircase winding its way up to the top floors.

The ballroom — and it was indeed a huge, wooden-floored ballroom complete with glittering chandeliers and a stage large enough to hold a full orchestra — was three flights up from the guest bedrooms. It was on the top floor, with what at one time had been a magnificent view of the surrounding city. Nowadays the view wasn't much to brag about, with the skyscrapers that had gone up blocking the river, but the ambiance and old charm still remained. Bob had taken care to have the entire house restored exactly as it had been in the early 1930s — with the exception of the extremely up-to-date security system he'd had installed. But the security system was nearly invisible. Stepping through the front doors was like going through a time warp.

And Bob was kind enough to share his beautiful home with Ellen and her kids for the summer.

Their summer of madness, she and Jamie and Lydia had called it back in Connecticut. They each had made a wish list of things they wanted to do while in the Big Apple for the summer. Jamie had wanted to visit the Museum of Natural History at least a dozen times and bum as many free tickets for as many Broadway shows as possible off of Bob, who was frequently sent comps. Lydia had wanted to shop for secondhand, ultrachic clothing in the Village, take jazz saxophone lessons with a real, live New York City jazz musician, and have at least one audition for a part in what she considered a *real* movie.

And Ellen . . . Ellen had wanted to leave her teaching job far, far behind, to check out the possibility of a career change, to investigate this acting thing that her kids had been doing so naturally for so long. She had wished for time to be totally selfish, to do things entirely for herself.

She'd gotten one hell of a jump on *that* part of it the night before, that was for darn sure.

Not only had she had an evening of totally hedonistic pleasure with a young, sexy, gorgeous man she barely knew, but she'd also allowed herself an after-midnight soak in her attached bathroom's Jacuzzi and a good, long, thoroughly selfish cry.

The kids had been asleep when she'd first gotten home, thank God, and she had crept up to her room feeling remarkably blue. It was odd, considering she'd spent most of the evening laughing.

Ellen hadn't been crying over Sam, that was for certain. For God's sake, she didn't know him well enough to cry over him. She'd told herself that enough times to be almost thoroughly convinced.

One thing she did know was that despite his dinner invitation and his attempt to get her phone number, she wasn't going to see Sam Schaefer ever again. She'd known that from the very start. In fact, that was one of the reasons she'd actually allowed herself to become intimate with him.

She wasn't ready for a real relationship right now, she told herself firmly. After Richard it was possible that she would never be ready again. But she'd known just from looking at Sam that he wasn't a real relationship kind of guy. He was a Romeo. A Lothario. A real ladies' man — in love with all women and no one woman.

Add to that part of the equation the fact that Ellen was nearly ten years his senior, and the solution was obvious — this was not a relationship that would work.

Not in a million years.

But together they'd had one incredible, passionate, perfect night.

Ellen gazed at the telephone. He wasn't going to call. She straightened her shoulders. And even if he did call and even if — and this was a ridiculous and impossible thing to suppose — even if Sam wanted a relationship with Ellen that would last more than a few hot, steamy, incredible nights, she would be a fool and a half to become involved with him.

In the first place, he was too much like

Richard. Handsome, charismatic, and probably just as incapable of fidelity. She'd been there. Done that.

In the second place, Ellen liked Sam too darn much. Unlike Richard, he had a solid sense of humor. He didn't take himself or life too seriously. He was irreverent and funny and quick to laugh at her jokes. He didn't humph and grump and say, "Be serious, Ellen," the way Richard used to do.

And he had all that gorgeous blond hair and those exquisite muscles.

No, she'd gotten exactly what she'd expected from Sam Schaefer — a single night of incredible lovemaking. A solid night of hot sex.

And her tears last night hadn't been because she'd known she wouldn't see him again. No, her tears had been from her sense of closure. Last night she'd finally put an end to her long, failed, farce of a marriage. She'd cried because she'd married Richard believing in forever, and she'd been betrayed by him most cruelly. She'd cried only because she'd been so very wrong.

Not because she wished she were ten years younger or Sam were ten years older. Not because she wished for something warm and loving and permanent with a stranger — something that would never be.

"Mom! Mom!" Lydia shrieked, bursting into the room. "I saw it! I saw it!"

Ellen knew instantly what her daughter was talking about. "The laundry detergent commercial! Oh my God! It's on?"

"It's *hysterical!*" Lydia danced around the room, stopping only to give her mother a hug. "You look *so good!* It was on one of the *networks,* on a *national* show. We are going to make *so* much money in residuals!"

Ellen laughed at her daughter's excitement. Fifteen-year-old Lydia was at the age where she downplayed everything, preferring to act ultracool. It was nice to see her jazzed, to hear her speaking in heavy italics, and to get a hug, however brief. Hugs from her nearly grown-up children were becoming more and more infrequent these days.

"You're just *so excellent,*" Lydia enthused. "I just *know* you're going to get that soap opera job after the producers see this."

"How about you?" Ellen interrupted. "You're in the commercial too."

Lydia shrugged that off. "I've done commercials before, it's no big deal for me, but for *you* . . . I had no clue you could act."

"Well, where do you think *you* got it from?" Ellen teased. "Certainly not your father."

Lydia rolled his eyes. "Daddy? He could be outacted by a plate of cottage cheese." She glanced at Ellen's appointment book, checking the information about the audition call that had come in. "Jamie said I've got something else for Monday?"

"Don't get excited — it's not a movie. It's a commercial."

Lydia pointed to Ellen's notes. "Does this say 'raisin bran'?"

"Yes, it does."

"Oh, blech," Lydia said. "I *hate* raisin bran." She smiled brightly, falsely. "But tomorrow I'll act like I absolutely *love* it."

"I hear you say that, and it frightens me. What exactly are you learning from these experiences?"

"Is that a rhetorical question, or do you really want me to answer that?" Lydia wondered.

The phone rang.

"I think it was rhetorical," Ellen said, "but think up a good answer in case I ask it again." She pushed the talk button on the phone. "Hello?"

"Got your phone number," a husky voice said. "But then again, I *am* a detective, I'm supposed to be able to track people down."

Ellen's heart lodged securely in her throat. "Sam?"

She looked up and directly into Lydia's curious dark brown eyes. "Sam?" her daughter mouthed silently, questioningly, unable to contain a smile. "Who's *Sam?*"

"I know you didn't want me to call you right away," Sam said apologetically, "but I haven't been able to stop thinking about you and —"

"I'm sorry," Ellen said. "Can you hold on for just a sec?" She covered the mouthpiece of the phone and moved toward the door, holding it open for Lydia. "May I please have some privacy?" she asked her daughter.

"Privacy," Lydia repeated, taking her sweet time to leave the room. "For *Sam.* No problem. Say hi to *Sam* for me."

Ellen closed the door. On second thought, she locked it. And then she moved far away, across to the other side of the room, in case Lydia had any ideas about eavesdropping.

"Sorry," she said. "I wasn't alone, and —"

"That's okay," he said in his too familiar, too sexy voice.

Ellen sat down on the window seat, closing her eyes at the sudden onslaught of extremely arousing memories. His hands, his mouth, his body . . .

"I was hoping you might've changed your mind about dinner tonight," he added.

"Oh," she said. "No." She took a deep

breath and lied. "I'm sorry, I've . . . I've got other plans and . . ."

"I've got tomorrow off," he said. "Maybe we could meet in the morning. Go for a run in Central Park before it gets too hot."

Ellen opened her eyes. "I didn't tell you that I like to run."

"You didn't have to," he said with a laugh. "You have a runner's legs. You have *gorgeous* legs — did I tell you that last night?"

"No," Ellen said weakly.

"Well, it's true. So what do you say I come by and pick you and your legs up around eight tomorrow morning?"

"I'm sorry," Ellen said again. "Sam, I just don't think —"

"I know I'm not giving you any time or space or whatever else it is you need to deal with your divorce, but I haven't been able to stop thinking about how perfectly we clicked last night, and, well, I really want to see you again."

Ellen was silent. She was facing the biggest temptation of her life. Sam wanted more. It was a possibility she hadn't seriously considered.

He wanted more, and she knew damn well that if she let this affair — if she could even call it that — go any further, *she* would be the one who would end up hurt. Because she knew exactly what would happen. She would see him tonight, tomorrow night, and for every night after that for a week or two. And then, just when she was starting to really care for him, just when she was starting to convince herself that the age difference wasn't really that huge, he would stop calling. And she'd spend the rest of the summer feeling like emotional roadkill.

She swore, sharply, pungently. "Sam, don't mess this up. Last night was perfect. If we add any more nights to it, it won't be perfect anymore."

He was silent for a moment. When he spoke, his voice was very quiet. "Are you telling me you don't want to see me again? Ever?"

"I think it would be better if we didn't," Ellen said. "See each other again. Yes. That's what I'm telling you." She closed her eyes again. Lord, she was doing this badly. But it was the right thing to do. She knew it was the right thing, the only thing — so why did she feel like crying?

"Oh," he said. His voice sounded so small. "I see. I'm sorry, I . . . guess I misunderstood."

"I'm sorry too," Ellen whispered. She was. She was very, *very* sorry.

He cleared his throat. "If you, uh . . . if

you change your mind, you know where to find me."

He hung up without saying good-bye, and for the second time in less than twelve hours, Ellen, who prided herself on her strength, who rarely ever cried, dissolved into tears.

T.S. gazed sympathetically at Sam over the rim of his coffee mug. "Okay," he said. "Answer this for me. Would you be as attracted to her if she hadn't rejected you?"

Sam had been staring sightlessly up at the television set playing silently in the corner of the little coffee shop, but now he looked over at his friend, outraged. "Yes," he said indignantly. "Jeez, what kind of a shallow, opportunistic bastard do you take me for?"

"The kind of shallow, opportunistic bastard who's never really felt the sting of rejection before," T.S. answered, not entirely unkindly.

"If you tell me I should take this as a learning experience, grow from it, and move on, I'm going to have to kill you," Sam said dangerously.

T.S. just laughed.

"God, I'm miserable." Sam pushed his cooling coffee away from him in disgust. "And you think it's funny."

"I'm dying to meet this woman," T.S. admitted, his light brown eyes amused behind his wire-rimmed glasses. "I'm having lunch with Bob after he gets back into town next week — Oh, I gave him a call and explained about the confusion at the airport. I had this fear that he was going to say 'You lied to me! I won't let you write my biography!' But he didn't. He thought it was funny that everyone thought you were me. He's going to think it's even funnier when he meets me — you and I are not exactly twins, white boy." He paused. "*Ellen* didn't think you were me when you . . . ?"

"No! No way. I told her who I really was right away."

"That's good."

"Yeah. So the book deal's final?"

"Contract's signed," T.S. told him. "There was even a write-up about it in the *Times.* Everyone's speculating that I'm going to go on Bob's show to promote the book."

"Are you?" Sam asked.

"Are you kidding?" T.S. snorted. He gestured around them at the little coffee shop as he lowered his voice. "Do you think I could sit here and have coffee with you if people knew I was T.S. Harrison?" He shook his head. "I love the fact that sixty million people have read my books, but I want to be able to walk my kids to school, thank you very much."

"Oh God," Sam breathed, staring transfixed at the TV screen. "There she is. Dammit, her commercial is on everywhere I go."

T.S. twisted in his seat to get a look at the TV.

On the small screen there was a close-up of Ellen, gazing into the camera and talking, her lips quirking upward into an almost smile. And then she *did* smile — right into the camera. Right into Sam's eyes, as if she were looking directly at him.

"She's an actress?" T.S. was confused. "Wait a minute, I thought you said she was a college professor."

"She's both," Sam told him, unable to tear his eyes away from the screen. Ellen held a bottle of laundry detergent and laughed with a young girl. It was uncanny — the girl they'd found to play her daughter looked almost exactly like her, with the exception of slightly darker hair.

"She's . . . not what I expected," T.S. said. "Somehow, from the way you were talking, I expected, I don't know, some total babe."

"She *is* a total babe — although, God, don't use that word around her. She's incredible, Toby," Sam told his friend as the commercial ended and he could once again drag his gaze away from the TV. "She makes me laugh. She's funny and sexy and . . ." He buried his head in his hands. "And she doesn't want to see me again."

T.S. shook his head. "I don't know what to tell you, man."

"I should feel relieved." Sam lifted his head and gripped the edge of the table. "I should be grateful — it was one really incredible night. I keep telling myself that she's doing me a huge favor by ending this thing before it even starts. And if it had been anybody else, *I* would've been the one talking from her side of the table. *I'm* the one who usually wants out of a relationship before it gets too heavy. How many times have I said those exact words she said to me?"

"By my estimation, four or five million?"

"Very funny."

"So now you know what it feels like to be dumped after one night," T.S. pointed out. "Welcome to the human race."

"It *sucks*."

"No kidding."

"I keep trying to figure out what I did wrong," Sam said. "But I didn't do anything wrong. We connected constantly, all night long. I mean, I know when it's working. You know me, Tobe, I'm *good* with women. I know when there's a certain magic there, and it was there, I'm telling you. So why would she run away from that?"

T.S. knew enough not to answer. He knew enough just to listen.

"I keep coming back to the same little piece of our conversation," Sam continued. "She asked if I had gone to NYU with you, and I told her I hadn't gone to college. I keep thinking maybe she thinks I'm not good enough for her — I'm not smart enough, not well educated enough."

"Oh, man, you don't really think that, do you?"

"I don't know what to think. You know, she teaches at *Yale.* She's got all these degrees dangling off her name. Doctor. She has a Ph.D. And me, I barely even finished high school."

T.S. sighed. "This is all my fault. If I hadn't agreed to meet Bob's aunt at the airport before I checked my calendar . . ."

They sat for a moment in silence, then Sam spoke. "No," he said quietly. "I would rather have met her than not."

"What are you going to do?"

Sam smiled grimly. "I'm going to figure out a way to see her again."

"Anything I can do to help?"

"Well, let's see," Sam said. "You're going

117

to be spending most of your time over the next few months hanging out at Bob Osborne's house — which happens to be where Ellen is living for the summer. Yes, my friend, I think you can probably help."

Six

"Excuse me, Bob, do you have a minute?" Ellen knocked on the half-opened door, poking her head into Bob's office. A large, handsome, African-American man — a stranger — was sitting across from his desk, and she instantly backed away. "Oh, I'm sorry, I didn't realize you were in a meeting."

"No, no." Bob waved her in from his prone position in his chair, feet up on his desk. "Come in. I want you to meet T.S. Harrison." He laughed. "The *real* T.S. Harrison."

Sam's best friend. How much had he told T.S., Ellen wondered as she forced a smile and shook the writer's hand. "I'm Ellen," she said.

T.S. was tall, taller than Sam, taller than Bob even, with a large frame that was on the verge of being beefy. His face was pleasantly round, his eyes a light shade of brown and magnified very slightly by a pair of stylishly old-fashioned wire-rimmed glasses. His hair was dark and curly and he wore it cut very short. He was dressed down in a gray NYU T-shirt and a pair of sweat-shorts.

Bob had on similar clothes. "We were just out shooting some hoops," he told her. "Did you know T.S. used to play basketball?"

"Actually," Ellen said, "I did know." She could feel T.S. watching her, still politely on his feet. "Please, sit down," she told him. She turned to Bob. "If this isn't a good time . . ."

Bob glanced at his watch. "No, we were just setting up an interview schedule — it's weird, for the next however many months I'm going to be talking to this kid about myself. I'm usually the one asking the questions." He looked at Ellen. "What's up?"

She sat down on the edge of the other chair positioned across from his desk, glancing briefly at T.S., who was still watching her. "Well, I couldn't help but notice when I got home a few minutes ago that we've gone to DefCon Three. I nearly had to get a retina scan to get past the men with guns who are guarding the doors. I expected them to hand me a clip-on photo ID. What's going on, Bob?"

"I upped security a little bit," Bob drawled.

"But you didn't call the police, did you?"

Bob wouldn't meet her eyes. "I didn't think it was nec—"

She stood up. "I knew you wouldn't. You're such a baby." She turned to T.S. "He probably didn't tell you what happened last night, either."

T.S. looked from Ellen to Bob. "What happened last night?"

"Nothing," Bob said.

"Nothing?" Ellen repeated. "The burglar alarm went off at two o'clock in the morning, waking us up and scaring the hell out of all of us. Even those of us who are pretending that it was nothing today."

"It was pretty exciting for a few minutes there," Bob agreed. "But my security team got it quickly under control."

"By finding out that someone hadn't broken in — they'd broken *out*," Ellen reminded him. "Someone was in here, some stranger was in this house when we all went to bed last night!"

"It happens sometimes," Bob said. "Some over-enthusiastic fan manages to sneak in, steals the hair from my hairbrush or something equally disgusting, and then leaves. It's no big deal."

"Don't you think it's just a little bit creepy considering the death threats you've been getting?"

T.S. sat up a little bit straighter. "*Death* threats?"

Bob pooh-poohed it. "Oh, I've gotten a few odd letters this past week. Nothing really that unusual. People are weirdos. And they think just because they can see me on their TV set every night that I'm talking directly to them. Some of them write back."

"What about those obscene phone calls?" Ellen asked. "How did they get your phone number?"

"That reminds me," Bob said to T.S. "I'm getting a new line. It's going to take a few days, but my number's going to change. Call Zoey, my assistant at the studio. She'll give you the new number when we find out what it's going to be."

"I don't know what to do — he won't call the police," Ellen said to T.S.

"He hates it when his favorite niece talks about him in the third person, as if he weren't in the room," Bob said loudly.

Ellen turned to her uncle. "Bobby, I want you to call the police. I don't want you to end up like John Lennon."

Bob sighed with exasperation. "Sweetie, I promise I'm being very careful. But I can't just call the police every time some nut wants a piece of me. I'm in contract negotiations with the network, and I don't want any negative publicity circulating for them to throw in my face. To be honest, every time I contact the police about some security problem, the incident shows up on the front page of *The Daily Star* — along with a sidebar that brings up my lurid past and a headline that suggests I've been drinking again." He shook his head in exasperation. "I don't need that right now."

T.S. cleared his throat. "I could give Sam a call."

Ellen froze.

"Who?" Bob asked.

"Sam," T.S. repeated. "Sam Schaefer. A friend of mine who's a police detective. He's the guy you met at the airport, picking up your aunt. You thought he was me? Remember, I was telling you about him just a little while ago. We were going to call him to come play b-ball with us tomorrow."

"Sam. Right. He's a cop? No kidding."

T.S. nodded. "He works out of the Twentieth Precinct — it's not too far from here. I'm sure he can be very discreet."

Bob pushed his telephone toward T.S. "Okay, call your friend. See if he'll come over and tell us exactly what we know —

that some nut's just trying to get a little attention." He turned to Ellen. "We'll all talk to T.S.'s friend Sam. Does that make you happy?"

"Um," said Ellen.

Sam heard the sound of Ellen's footsteps out on the marble tile of the entrance hall and he took a deep breath, trying to slow his accelerated heartbeat.

He couldn't believe his luck. He and T.S. had been thinking for days, trying to come up with a way to finagle an extra invitation to dinner at Bob Osborne's, and wham, this opportunity seemed to fall into their laps. Crank phone calls and a couple of negative letters from some disgruntled crackpot. It was surely nothing to worry about, yet it gave him one damn fine excuse to be sitting in Bob Osborne's living room, about to see Ellen Layne again.

"Here comes Ellen now," Bob said. "She and Lydia are the ones who've gotten the nasty phone calls. Jamie and I have both answered the phone and had the caller hang up — it's happened too often to be a wrong number."

Jamie and Lydia. Bob had mentioned those names before, but Sam hadn't had a chance to inquire. Other people must be living here besides Bob and Ellen.

And then Ellen appeared, and Sam forgot about everything else. She was wearing jeans shorts, cuffed at the bottom, a T-shirt that managed both to cover her thoroughly and look utterly sexy, and sneakers. Her gleaming reddish blond hair was pulled back into a ponytail.

She looked gorgeous.

She didn't quite meet Sam's eyes. Instead she smiled vaguely in his direction as she moved soundlessly now across the deep reds and blues of the Persian carpet that stretched over the wide living room floor.

"Ellen, you remember Sam, don't you?" Bob said.

"Of course." She turned toward Sam and forced a smile.

Sam stood up, holding out his hand to shake, and she had to take it.

"How are you?" she asked politely, hesitating only slightly before slipping her fingers into his.

Her hand was warm and faintly damp, cluing him in to her nervousness. He held on to it longer than he knew he should, but dammit, he didn't want to let her go. "Actually, this past week has been just short of hell."

She looked up at him then, *really* looked

into his eyes. "I'm so sorry to hear that," she murmured.

She was embarrassed — he could tell. She was embarrassed and uncomfortable to see him again after what they'd done in that limo a little over a week ago.

God, how often had *he* been the one who was embarrassed when he ran into some woman with whom he'd had only the briefest of encounters and then hadn't bothered to call again?

But there was more than embarrassment in her eyes. There was attraction too. It was unmistakable. He knew just from looking that the spark was still there. He knew without a doubt that once hadn't been enough for her either. So why was she pretending it had been?

"Did Bob show you the letters?" she asked, extracting her hand from his. "The death threats?"

"I thought I'd let you do that," Bob said, standing up and all but tossing a manila file folder at her. "You're the one who thinks there's a problem. I've got to head over to the studio."

Bob was leaving. Sam and Ellen would soon be alone. Sam's luck was definitely starting to change.

Ellen blocked Bob's path. "You can't just

leave!" There was a trace of panic in her voice.

"Of course I can," her uncle told her cheerfully. "You and Lydia are the ones who got the phone calls. *You're* the one who thinks there's a real problem — the one who wanted Detective Schaefer to come out here in the first place. I'm the one who thinks I've just temporarily captured the attention of some weirdo who will quickly lose interest in me just as soon as Paris Hilton comes back to town."

"But, Bob —"

He kissed her on the cheek. "I have to go to work." He turned to Sam. "If you have any questions, call me at the studio. Oh, and also feel free to talk to Tran Minh Hyunh, my security chief. She's going to be here at home all day, running a test on the security system. Maybe between the two of you, you can convince the worrywart here that there's nothing to be afraid of." He stepped around Ellen and breezed out of the room. "See you later, kids."

Ellen stood clutching the file folder, staring after her uncle. As his footsteps faded into the distance she turned and smiled weakly at Sam. "Well. This is awkward."

"It's nice to see you again, Ellen," Sam said quietly.

In some ways it was nice to see him again too. He looked delicious. He was dressed almost exactly the same as he had been the night they'd met. Jeans, sneakers, sport jacket, white shirt, tie. Only this time he was carrying a gun. She'd caught a glimpse of it beneath his jacket as he'd leaned forward to shake her hand.

He smelled good too. The faint scent of his cologne brought back sudden vivid memories that she desperately tried to banish from her mind. His mouth and hands, touching, kissing. The smooth, hard muscles of his back beneath her palms. His body filling her . . .

"This is *very* awkward," she said again as she tossed the file folder down on a coffee table and sat on the plush golden-colored sofa. "For the record, it was T.S.'s idea to call you. There wasn't much I could do to stop him, short of asking if he wouldn't mind calling a different detective. I mean, there must be at least a thousand New York City police detectives that I *haven't* slept with."

Sam laughed at her blunt honesty as he sat down some distance from her on the couch. " 'Of all the gin joints in all the towns in all the world she walks into mine,' " he quoted from *Casablanca*. "It's not really coincidental, though. Or even fate. As far as I know, I'm the only cop T.S. knows. You and I were destined to meet again." He paused. "God knows I've been running into you often enough on my television set."

Ellen couldn't help feeling a flash of pleasure. "You've seen the commercial?"

He smiled into her eyes. "Yeah, I've seen it. About four hundred times. It's great. Every time it comes on, I'm mesmerized. You're incredibly photogenic."

His eyes were much too warm and she had to look away. "Thank you." She opened the file folder on the coffee table. "You're here on business — we should probably get to it."

"I've got time," he told her.

She glanced at him, remembering what had happened the last time he'd told her that. She pushed the file with the letters in his direction, choosing to ignore his softly spoken words. "This is the latest file of what Bob calls 'questionable' mail."

Sam gazed at her as he pulled the opened file closer, but it was clear she wasn't going to look back at him again. So he looked at the file.

The letters — if you could call them letters — were drawn in crayon on white lined loose-leaf notebook paper, but other than that, there was nothing childish about them. Sam flipped through the pages quickly. From what he could see, there were three different letters, each separately paper-clipped, each several pages long. They all had a similar last page — a rather expertly drawn picture of eyes and words printed in block letters in black crayon: "I am watching you."

It was decidedly creepy.

"The first one is on the bottom," Ellen told him. "It arrived just about a week ago, on June twenty-eighth. I remember because Lydia had a callback that day."

Sam nodded, looking at that one first. He took a small notebook from his jacket pocket and scribbled a few notes. "Did these all come in the mail?"

"Death" was the only word on the first page, and the picture was a rather graphically drawn illustration of death by gunshot. Whoever had drawn this was quite an artist, particularly considering he or she was using only crayons. The victim was grimacing as bullets exploded through his chest. *Her* chest? It was hard to tell, actually.

The second page said "Life," and it showed what looked to be rather hideously drawn creatures — angels maybe? — holding an unconscious or limp person whose head was down and toes were dragging, carrying him or her — again it was hard to tell — up to the clouds.

The second letter had the same words, but different illustrations. "Death," or "Deth" this time — it was spelled wrong on this page — showed a contorting figure being burned alive by fire. "Life" was more of those grotesque angels. And then there were the eyes. "I am watching you."

"The first two arrived by mail," Ellen told him. "They were kind of odd. There was no name on the envelopes, just the address. The third one was taped to the front door. Jamie found it day before yesterday. That was, let's see . . . July first."

Sam looked up at her. "Do you have the envelopes?"

She shook her head. "If they're not in that file, then no."

"And you're sure Bob's name wasn't on any of the envelopes? Not anywhere?"

"They only had the address. The one that was taped to the door didn't have anything written on it at all."

"And they were sent here, to the house, not to the studio?"

"That's right."

"If you get anything else like this either in

the mail or hand delivered, make sure you save the envelopes," he said.

Ellen nodded. "Isn't this really creepy?" she asked, using the exact same word he'd been thinking. "I mean, they're not exactly death threats, but there is some kind of threat implied, isn't there?"

"Yeah," Sam agreed. "I'd say *something's* implied."

The third letter was different. There were only two pages. The first was a picture of the awful angels. Underneath the crayon drawing were the words "They are watching me." The second was the eyes again, and the words "I am watching you."

"You said Jamie found this taped to the door?"

Ellen nodded.

"Bob mentioned Jamie too — and someone named Lydia. Do they live here too? Are they, like, hired help?"

Ellen laughed. And laughed. For some reason, she found his question very funny. "They are, in fact, nothing like hired help," she told him. "I can ask them to come down here if you want to talk to them."

"Yeah, I'll want to do that, but first I have some questions about the phone calls. Can you tell me about how many you've received?"

"I've gotten at least three. Lydia got one. I no longer allow her or Jamie to answer the phone."

Sam looked up at her over the pages of his notebook. "Allow?"

She smiled at him sweetly, almost sadly. "Lydia and Jamie are my children, Sam."

Children? Shock spread through him in waves. She hadn't mentioned her kids even once the entire time they were together. "You didn't tell me you had kids."

"Well, I do. A fifteen-year-old daughter and a thirteen-year-old son."

"Why didn't you tell me?"

"You didn't ask."

"There're a lot of things I didn't ask."

Ellen shifted in her seat, clearly ill at ease. Why hadn't she told him about her kids? Had she intended to deceive him from the very start? Had she planned to seduce him? Had she planned to use him for only one night of pleasure, and therefore hadn't bothered to tell him more about herself than the information she'd had to provide to answer his questions? Hell, if she were that calculating, she damn well could've lied about *everything*.

"Do you want me to tell you about the phone calls?" she asked.

Sam's voice sounded harsh even to his

own ears, but he couldn't stop himself. "No, I want to know what else you didn't tell me. Are you really divorced, or is Richard hiding somewhere upstairs too?"

Ellen sat silently, staring at the floor, and Sam cursed softly. "I'm sorry," he said.

She looked up at him, her brown eyes vulnerable and so very sad. "No, I probably deserved that." She stood up. "Maybe you should go."

Sam didn't stand up. Instead he picked up the file of letters and sighed.

"No, I shouldn't go. You've got a problem here," he said, gesturing to the file, "that's bigger than this problem here," he added, gesturing between the two of them. "Please, sit down and tell me about the phone calls."

Ellen sat down slowly, her eyes searching his face. "You think this could be serious?"

"Bob said something about a caller hanging up when he and Jamie picked up the phone. Have I got it right? You and your daughter were the only ones who've gotten these calls?"

Ellen nodded.

"Can you tell me everything you remember about the calls? Can you describe the voice?"

"Male," she said, her eyes still on his face. "It was definitely a man, even though it was kind of high pitched and raspy, as if he were trying to disguise his voice."

"What did he say?"

"It was weird. The first time I picked up the phone, he said something like, 'Do you like to fly?' and I said something like, 'Who is this?' or 'Who's calling?' He asked something else really odd — 'What do you smell like?' or, no, 'Who do you smell like?' It was weird. Who. And then he said — and I remember this really clearly, because he said the same thing in the other calls, and to Lydia too. He said, 'Do you want to get probed too? Where do you want to get probed?' " Her face flushed and she glanced away from him. "And then he got pretty explicit with his list of choices. That's when I hung up."

Sam was scribbling her words down in his notebook. Probed. That wasn't a word he'd heard too often. Maybe they'd get lucky and come up with a match for some previously apprehended creep's MO. They'd plug the words used in both the phone calls and the letters into the police computer — together and separately, because at this stage they couldn't even assume it was the same guy — hoping to find some previously tagged sex offender with a similar method of operation. This kind of creep tended to favor certain words over others, such as "probe," or asking *who* you smell like, rather than *what,* and those word choices sometimes helped in identifying them.

And IDing this guy would help them find him.

"The second and third times he called, I hung up as soon as he started talking about probes," Ellen continued.

Sam looked up. "Did he ask for or mention your uncle at all?"

"No."

He flipped back through his pages of notes. "The first letter arrived on . . . June twenty-eighth. The first phone call was . . . before that or after that?"

"After. A couple days after."

"You're certain of that?"

"Yes. I'm sure you know that Bob's number is unlisted. He thought it was just a coincidence. But I remember being really spooked, thinking it was maybe the same guy who sent those awful pictures. Still, Bob thought it was just some pervert who randomly dialed a number, searching for a female voice.

Sam glanced up from his notes.

"But you don't think that, do you?" Ellen

asked, a note of worry creeping into her voice.

He shook his head. "Ellen, do you remember the date your commercial first aired?"

She frowned. "No. Wait — yes. It was . . ." She met his gaze only briefly. "It was the day after us. You know. You, me, the lions . . ."

Sam smiled crookedly. "I don't need a lot of reminding about that." He flipped through his notebook to a calendar page. "That was a week ago Friday. So you saw the commercial on Saturday . . . June twenty-fifth." He looked up at Ellen. "Three days before you got the first threatening letter — sent to this address, without a specific name on the envelope."

He held out the drawings of the victim in the pictures labeled "Death." "Look at the hair color," he continued. "That's not Bob. Bob has dark hair. In both of these pictures, this person is blond."

"Oh my God. Do you think . . . ?"

"I think these letters weren't for Bob," Sam said grimly. "Ellen, I think they were meant for *you.*"

SEVEN

"Mr. Harrison! How are you, sir? Nice to see you again."

Sam looked up to see Ron, the limo driver, waving to him from where the stretch limousine was parked in front of Bob Osborne's house.

"You mind if we take a second to set this guy straight?" he asked T.S. He didn't wait for his friend to respond before approaching Ron and holding out his hand for a shake. "Hey, how's it going, Ron?"

"Fine, thank you, sir."

"Look," Sam said, "I wanted to introduce someone to you." He turned to T.S. "This is —"

"Tobias Shavar," T.S. interrupted, reaching past him to shake Ron's hand. "I'm Mr. Harrison's assistant."

"Nice meeting you, Tobias," Ron said. "I'm a big fan of your boss."

"Mr. Harrison *is* a brilliant writer," T.S.

agreed, with a broad grin in Sam's direction. "He is without a doubt one of the true American geniuses."

Sam knew T.S. well enough to know there was a reason he'd kept Ron in the dark about their real identities. He waited until they were far enough away, heading up the stairs to the front door of Bob's town house, before he quietly asked, "You want to tell me what the hell that was about?"

"I figured out the perfect plan," T.S. told him smugly.

"Well, you are an American genius — you said so yourself," Sam said snidely. "Are you going to tell me, or are you going to use your brilliant mental powers to send this perfect plan to me telepathically?"

Before either of the men hit the bell, the door swung open and a bespectacled little boy gazed out at them. "Sorry," the kid said. "We just bought Girl Scout cookies from the kid down the street." He started to swing the door closed, then opened it again, laughing at the expression on their faces. "I'm kidding. I know you're not Girl Scouts — I could tell because you're not wearing green skirts. You're T.S. Harrison and his friend, right?" He pointed first to T.S. and then to Sam. "T.S.? Or T.S.?"

They both pointed to Sam and said in

unison, "T.S."

"I'm Tobias Shavar," T.S. said. Sam glanced over at his friend. T.S. was enjoying this false identity thing a little too much. But then again, T.S. had always been a big fan of intrigue.

"They're waiting for you in Bob's office," the kid said, opening the door wider to let them in.

"You've got to be Ellen's kid," Sam said as he stepped into the entry hall.

He was surprised. "You know my mom?"

"Yeah, I do," Sam said. "You must be Jamie."

An armed security guard stood on the other side of the door, watching them expressionlessly. Sam nodded to the man and got an almost imperceptible nod back.

"James," the kid said in a haughty English accent. "I'm the butler-in-training. I've been sent to escort you upstairs. This way, gentlemen."

The kid looked to be about ten, but his attitude and his sense of humor were that of a much older child. His eyes were blue, and his hair was light brown and gelled to stand up straight, as if his finger were permanently stuck in a light socket. Sam searched for Ellen in the boy's face and found her in the slight pointedness of his chin, and in the

140

way his lips seemed to quirk upward in an expression of permanent amusement.

As they took the elevator up to the second floor, Sam met T.S.'s eyes. "The plan?" he asked quietly.

T.S. gazed at the kid, who stared back at them in unabashed curiosity. "You're writing Bob's biography," T.S. said to Sam. "So you have a reason to be here, right?"

Just like that, Sam understood the plan. It was crazy.

"So do it," T.S. said. "Have free run of the place, even move in if you want to, arouse no suspicions, catch you-know-who . . . and maybe even achieve a few of your own personal goals at the same time."

The elevator door opened and Jamie — *James* — stepped haughtily out. "This way, sirs."

"We'll catch up to you in a sec, kid." Instead of following Jamie down the hall, Sam stopped, drawing T.S. back, and said in a lowered voice, "In theory it works."

"Why not in reality?" T.S. asked.

Sam didn't want to say the words aloud. This was something he hadn't talked even to T.S. about. This was behind all of his soul-searching of late. This was the reason he was considering leaving the police force.

He was afraid he wasn't good enough. He

was afraid he couldn't get the job done.

This whole scenario was too similar to last year's assignment that had gone horribly wrong. Sam had been entrusted to protect a witness who was due to testify in court against a well-connected mobster. But the entire situation had gone to hell in a hand-basket. While moving the witness to the courthouse from a supposedly secret location at a supposedly safe house, two detectives and the witness had been shot and nearly killed. Sure, Sam had come up clean in the ensuing investigation. According to the report by Internal Affairs, everyone had agreed that Sam had done all that he could to prevent the attack. One of the other detectives from his precinct — a man he'd had no reason to mistrust — had betrayed them. There was no way Sam could have known.

But he *should* have known. So, in a very real sense, Sam was entirely to blame.

He couldn't stop thinking that somehow — maybe if he were a better cop — he should have known. If he had had his father's and his grandfather's instincts, he would have known. He should have been able to look out at the street and *know* that there was going to be an attempt to hit the witness. His father would've known. But that cop's special sixth-sense gene hadn't been carried down to Sam.

And now here he was, on the verge of facing a situation where he would be called upon to protect a woman that he cared very much about, a woman that he wanted desperately to have a relationship with.

He was already emotionally involved — that alone was a good enough reason to stay the hell away from this case. In fact, he was the last guy who should take this on. He should spill his guts to his precinct's lieutenant and have someone else assigned to protect Ellen.

But what if Autweiler or Janowski were assigned to the case? Or, damn, how about Artie Medner? As incompetent as Sam feared he himself was, he knew those three bozos were just cruising along, waiting for retirement. Never mind the fact that Autweiler had a good fifteen years to go before he could even begin thinking about a pension.

No, as much as Sam didn't want to be responsible for Ellen's safety, he couldn't think of a single man or woman to whom he'd want to hand over the job of protecting her.

God help him, though. He wasn't going to sleep until they caught this guy.

"Man, I would've thought you would've jumped at a chance like this," T.S. said, his eyes narrowing as he gazed at Sam.

"This is a serious situation, Toby. There's a very real threat. It's not some game. This is no longer about me trying to get close to Ellen."

T.S. lowered his voice even further. "You're scared, aren't you?"

Sam nodded, although T.S. would never know just how very much he was afraid. "I could be wrong, but I think the guy who sent those letters and made those phone calls is dead serious. I think he wants to kill Ellen." He took a deep breath and exhaled hard. "So let's go in there and convince Bob and Ellen to go along with your plan, so I can start making damn sure she stays safe."

Please God, he added silently, *don't let me mess this up.*

"You don't think the person who's stalking Ellen is one of our household staff, do you?" Bob asked, concern in his voice. He was no longer shrugging off the threatening notes — not now that it looked as if Ellen were the intended target. He could be flip about his own safety, but not about hers.

"He's not one of the guys in my security team, that's for sure," Hyunh said flatly.

"I've got three men who've been with me for four years. I trust them."

Bob's security chief, Tran Minh Hyunh, was a diminutive Vietnamese woman who had worked for him for the past ten years — and possibly even longer. Despite the gray that ran through her long, dark braid, Hyunh was entirely capable of taking out a gang of the toughest street thugs without having to catch her breath. Ellen knew this because she'd seen the security chief working out with the rest of her team in Bob's gym. She'd thrown men who were more than twice her size with seemingly little effort.

"I think the stalker could be connected to someone who knows Bob quite well," Sam said. "This guy has access to Bob Osborne's unlisted telephone number, remember. Of course, there are other ways he could have gotten that, but at this point I wouldn't want to assume anything."

"I think it would be smart not to let anyone outside of this room know that Sam isn't really me," T.S. pointed out.

"My security team needs to know," Hyunh said. "But they'll be discreet."

Ellen looked around the room from Bob to Hyunh to T.S. and finally to Sam. "There's no way we can keep all this from

145

Lydia and Jamie," she said.

"Can they keep a secret of this magnitude?" Bob wondered.

"I'm not sure I understand exactly why they'd have to," Ellen countered.

"It would be best if we could keep my identity from the staff," Sam explained. "The stalker could know one of them, or he could just be someone who knows where to go to overhear staff members' private conversations. Whatever the case, the last thing we want him to do is find out that a cop has moved into the house. We want to nail this guy. We don't want him to get spooked and back away. We don't want him to disappear on us only to reappear later when Ellen's not expecting it."

Ellen felt dizzy. This was about *her*. Someone had seen her commercial and now they wanted to kill her. She laughed, her voice sounding a touch hysterical. She didn't think her acting was *that* bad. She looked up to find Sam watching her, his crystal blue eyes totally devoid of humor.

Both he and Bob had been talking in slightly hushed, grim tones, as if she were already dead. They were making plans for Sam to move in — *move in?* Ellen nearly fell out of her chair as the meaning of their words sunk in. Move in *here?* Into the same house that she was living in?

This so-called plan was totally insane. She could barely sit in the same room with Sam Schaefer, let alone live in the same house with him for the next however many weeks it took to catch this stalker.

Ellen knew without a shadow of a doubt that she had been right in her painful decision not to see Sam again. Because seeing him again was drawing her attention to all those little things about him that she'd liked so much — and tried so hard to forget. His kindness. His quick sense of humor. The sweetness in his eyes — a sweetness that both complemented and contrasted with the heat that lingered there, just below the surface. That soft blond hair that fell forward into his eyes. The hard muscles of his shoulders and arms that flexed and shifted with his every slight movement. That smile that was as sexy as sin.

But she couldn't forget how quiet and subdued he'd become when she'd told him she didn't want to see him again. And she couldn't forget the flash of hurt she'd seen in his eyes more than once since he'd been over here today.

Was it really hurt that glimmered there? Or was it merely damaged pride? He'd called her, probably expecting her to be panting to see him again. He'd probably expected her to be grateful that he'd called, and eager for another chance to fall into his arms.

Instead she'd turned him down.

But what he didn't know was that she'd turned him down because she was afraid that if she saw him again, she would do something really stupid — like fall in love with him.

"I think I'll just go home." Ellen stood up. "I'll just pack the kids up and we'll go back to Connecticut. It's the obvious solution."

But both Bob and Sam were shaking their heads.

"No," Bob said. "What's to keep this guy from following you?"

"Believe it or not," Sam added, "you're safest right here. This place is a fortress. This security system is one of the best private systems I've ever seen. Unless you have a similar one on your house in Connecticut . . . ?"

He knew damn well that she didn't.

"I have an extra dead bolt on my front door," she told him. "And a sawed-off broom handle stuck in the runner of the sliding glass door in the playroom. That's the extent of my security system at home."

"Leaving here isn't an alternative," Bob told her firmly.

"What am I supposed to do?" she said, her voice rising with frustration. "Spend the rest of the summer locked inside this house, scared to death, waiting for some Anthony Perkins wannabe to grab me while I'm in the shower?"

"It'll be my job to make sure that you're neither scared to death nor locked in the house," Sam told her. "And with the new adjustments Hyunh's made to the security system, the incident that occurred — when someone was locked in the house with you for the night — will not be repeated. Believe me, no one will be able to grab you while you're in the shower." He held her gaze unswervingly, a slight smile playing about the corners of his mouth. "Unless you want them to."

Ellen felt herself blush as Sam turned back to Bob.

"I'll want to dust for fingerprints in the room the intruder was in," he continued. "I'll want to take a look at the window he used to exit the house. And I'd like you to delay getting your phone number changed. I want to set up a system to tape and try to trace these phone calls — although I wouldn't be surprised if this guy uses a pay phone."

Sam looked at Ellen. "I'll need to talk to your kids and explain why they need to keep all this a secret. And we'll need to set up some ground rules for when they want to leave the house."

"I don't let them go out into the city alone," Ellen told him. "They're either with me or Bob or Hyunh if they go outside."

"That's good," he said. "Then it won't be as if we're suddenly putting all these restrictions on them." He smiled at her reassuringly. "Don't look so worried. This is going to be okay. I promise."

He looked so capable, so solid, so totally in control as he smiled at her that way. This is going to be okay? That was what worried her. Ellen was afraid that this was going to be just a little *too* okay.

She had a sudden vision of Sam, in her bed, holding her safe in the circle of his arms as they slept through the darkest hours of the night. She had a vision of him making absolutely sure that no one grabbed her in the shower — because he was in there with her, water pounding on their bodies as he kissed her and . . .

Ellen stood up and cleared her throat. Maybe if she acted absolutely cool, he'd

150

believe that she intended to keep their relationship strictly one of business from now on. Maybe if she kept her distance, she'd believe it too.

"Why don't you come with me, Detective? I'll introduce you to Lydia and Jamie."

"We have a suite of rooms up on the third floor," Ellen continued as Sam followed her out into the hall and toward the marble staircase. Everything about her — her tone of voice, the way she was walking, the formal set of her head — was that of a tour guide rather than a lover. Former lover. Past tense. It was more than clear that Ellen had no intention of reprising that role.

Sam felt a flood of frustration. What had he done that was so wrong? What had he said to make her so certain that she didn't want a relationship with him?

The sex had been great. He had no doubts about that. But even he knew that physical compatibility wasn't enough to base a relationship upon. And the sex wasn't the reason why he'd been so intent upon seeing her again. Well, okay, in all honesty, it did have something to do with it. In fact, he'd wanted desperately to make love to Ellen again from the moment he'd stepped out of that limousine, a week ago Friday. But even more than he'd wanted that, he'd wanted the easy company, the laughter, the friendship they'd shared.

"Ellen, before we talk to your kids, I was wondering . . ." Sam saw her stiffen at his words, and he felt a flare of impatience. "What? Did you think I was going to ask if you wouldn't mind slipping into the linen closet to get it on with me? Jeez," he exhaled in frustration. "You know, I may not be the smartest guy in the world, but I'm not a complete idiot. As much as I'd like to occupy the same three square feet of confined space with you again, give me a *little* credit to recognize what's appropriate and what's not, considering I'm working and your kids are around."

She flushed. "I'm sorry. I'm . . . a little tense."

"I noticed. I was wondering if it was humanly possible for you to clench your teeth more tightly together," he told her. "You're so tense, *I'm* getting a headache."

That produced a wan smile.

Ellen was really freaked out about this whole stalker situation. And being forced to see *him* again was only making it worse. She stood there, in the hall, arms folded across her chest as if holding on to herself, and

Sam felt the sharpness of his frustration melt into something warmer, something sadder. She looked so vulnerable. He wanted to put his arms around her and comfort her, but he knew that touching her was the last thing she'd want him to do.

Instead he made himself smile. "Hey," he said. "Lighten up, all right? The stalker's the guy who's hassling you, not me. I'm the good guy, okay?"

She nodded. "I know you are."

"Okay," he said. "Now, what I was going to ask was whether you thought it would be all right if we told your kids the entire truth about what's happening here — about the death threats and everything. I don't want to scare them, but it's important that they know why they're absolutely not allowed to leave this house alone."

Ellen nodded again. "Yeah, I think we should tell them, but maybe downplay the fact that this guy could be after me. I mean, we don't really know that. He could be after Bob." Her sense of humor made an attempt at a comeback. "He *should* be after Bob, what with those tacky dumb blond jokes he made on his show last night. Lord, after that, I'm tempted to dye my hair back to its regular color."

"Maybe you should."

"Are you serious?"

Sam smiled ruefully. "People — especially crazy people — fixate on the strangest things. It's possible that without blond hair, you won't be the lady in the detergent commercial anymore — at least not to the stalker. He may lose interest."

"Or he might immediately kill the evil brunette imposter for taking the place of his blond goddess."

Sam laughed. "And then there's always that possibility."

"No, I think I want to catch this guy," Ellen said. "If we don't catch him, I'm going to spend the rest of my life checking over my shoulder, too spooked to stay home alone. I'll have to move into the freshmen dorm with Jamie when he goes to college. Something tells me he won't be too happy about that."

We. She'd said, "If *we* don't catch him." It was only one little word, but it made Sam happier than he'd been in over a week. *We.* He liked the way that sounded. "We'll catch him," he said. God help him, he would make damn sure of it — if it was the last thing he ever did.

Ellen took a deep breath, risking another

glance up at Sam. He was gazing at her, his eyes much too warm. She started to walk again, heading down the long hallway toward Jamie's and Lydia's bedrooms. She could hear the familiar sounds of her children — Jamie's Super Nintendo and Lyd's saxophone. Fortunately, this old house was well soundproofed or they would have heard them down in Bob's office too.

"Hey, Lyd," she said, knocking on her daughter's door. "There's someone here I want you to meet."

Lydia came to the door, her alto sax still attached to her neck strap. She had that hostile, don't-bother-me-now look in her eyes, but it faded almost instantly when she caught sight of Sam.

"Whoa," she said, gazing at him with her usual lack of shyness. "Who are you?"

"Wait a minute," Sam said to Ellen. "This is the girl from the commercial."

"Yeah," Ellen told him. "She's my daughter, Lydia." She turned to Lydia. "This is Sam Schaefer."

"Sam," Lydia repeated, the last of her hostility vanishing as she gave her mother a questioning look, a look filled with silent messages. "This is Sam? Phone call Sam?"

"He's a detective with the New York City police," Ellen told her.

"A detective? No way!"

"Way," Ellen said. "He needs to talk to you and Jamie."

Lydia looked from Ellen to Sam and back again. "Why? Is something wrong?"

Sam gazed at Ellen's daughter. She looked like Ellen only skinnier and smaller. She was a cute version of Ellen's grown-up beauty. Her hair was longer and light brown, her eyes the same dark chocolate color as Ellen's. But she didn't smile half as much. Of course, lately, Ellen wasn't smiling too often either.

But man, this complicated things. Sam didn't even know for sure that the stalker was after Ellen and not Bob, and now they could throw Lydia, also a possible target, into the celebrity pot.

"You didn't tell me Lydia was an actress too," he said.

"Actor," Lydia corrected him with a stern look. "It's sexist to say 'actress.' "

"Sorry."

"She's the reason I was in the right place at the right time for that commercial," Ellen told him.

Sam nodded. He remembered her telling him that was how she'd won the part.

"Lyd got the part of the daughter, and I went with her into the city for the shoot.

The actress — actor," she quickly corrected herself with a glance at Lydia, "who was cast as the mother was a no-show. It turns out she was in a serious car accident, but we didn't know it at the time. The director's assistant was running around trying to find out what had happened to her, and I stood in for the mother during one of the rehearsals to help Lyd out with her blocking. The director liked what I did, and the rest is history."

"Have you seen the commercial?" Lydia asked Sam.

"Yes, I have."

"Isn't Mom cute in it? It's her first one."

"Yes, she's very cute," he said, glancing at Ellen. She was working hard to ignore his words. "How many commercials have you done?" he asked Lydia.

She shrugged. "I don't know. A half a dozen local spots — you know, nonunion work. And in the past few years, I've had three SAG jobs — which is really good since I don't live in New York City."

Sam looked at Ellen. "SAG?"

"Screen Actors Guild," she interpreted.

"Oh."

"Jamie's done even more than me," Lydia told him. "That's because he still looks like a little twerpy kid. He can do a great whining nine-year-old."

Sam turned to Ellen again. "Jamie does commercials too?"

She nodded. "As a matter of fact, we all have an audition tomorrow at the same casting agency. Although at this point I'm considering canceling."

"What?" Lydia's voice went up an octave. "Why?"

"You don't have to cancel," Sam told her. "If you change your plans, if you let yourself be intimidated, then this guy automatically wins."

"*What* guy?" Lydia asked.

"Please go find Jamie," Ellen asked her daughter, "and meet us in the yellow room? I'll explain what's going on."

EIGHT

"I can't believe I've been living here in this house and I didn't have a clue any of this was going on," Lydia lamented. "I mean, I knew about that gross phone call, but other than that, I've been drifting around here, totally serene."

"I knew everything," Jamie announced.

"That's 'cause you're a twerp."

"*I'm* a twerp? I don't think so, butthead."

"I *hate* when you call me that!"

"I know. Butthead."

"Excuse me," Ellen said loudly. "You're both twerps and buttheads, okay? Or at least you will be if you keep acting like this. Just stop the fighting, all right?"

"Yeah," Jamie said. "This is like that *Star Trek* episode where the Klingons are suddenly beamed aboard the *Enterprise,* and this really tacky special effect light-being feeds off of all the fighting, and Captain Kirk and the Klingon commander have to pretend to be friends to make the alien go away."

"You mean 'The Day of the Dove'?" Lydia snorted. "It's nothing like that at all. It's much more like the really spooky one where the spirit of Jack the Ripper gets into the *Enterprise*'s computer and —"

"Nope," Ellen interrupted. "It's like 'The Corbomite Maneuver' — the episode where the really scary alien's face on the view screen turns out to be no one more dangerous than little Clint Howard with a bald wig on. The terrible threat is nothing more than a bluff, and everyone sits around at the end drinking tranya and laughing. *That's* what this is going to be like."

Sam was trying very hard not to laugh. Ellen glanced at him and couldn't keep her own smile from slipping out. For the briefest of moments, she forgot and she let herself gaze into his eyes. The connection was instant, but it was more than just molten-hot. It was warm too. And it was terribly hard to look away.

But she did, shaken by the weakness of her resolve, ashamed at how much she still wanted this man. When she looked at him again, she forced herself to focus on his gorgeous face, the casual perfection of his hair, the width of his shoulders.

She may have wanted him, but that wasn't a sign of weakness on her part. Ellen couldn't blame herself for being human. No woman alive between the ages of one and one hundred wouldn't have wanted Sam Schaefer in one way or another.

No one was immune to his charisma. Not even Lydia. He'd managed to wrap Ellen's perpetually bored daughter totally around his little finger.

Ellen watched as Sam spoke to both Lydia and Jamie, giving them the list of rules they were going to follow to ensure everyone's safety until the stalker was caught. Jamie was listening intently — that was no surprise. He was still young enough to have a sense of unreality about the entire situation. To him this was nothing more than a giant game. She knew that over the next few days she'd find him slinking about the house, playing detective — baseball cap pulled down low over his eyes, water pistol clutched in his hand as he peered out the windows, looking for any sign of someone watching the house.

Ellen made a mental note to make sure the water pistol stayed empty. Bob would definitely *not* be into Jamie dripping water on his expensive antiques.

"Do you have any questions?" Sam asked

her children.

Lydia, ever the actor, was playing the part of the complete, concerned grown-up. "I just made arrangements to take lessons from Casey Redmond, the sax player from Bob's house band. We were going to meet at his place, across town. Should I ask him to come here instead?"

"Definitely." Sam took out his notebook, making note of the name.

Lydia was fascinated. "You don't think it could be Casey, do you?"

"Right now I only know that it's not you or Jamie or Ellen or Bob or me or T.S. or Hyunh and her security team, but that's where my list ends. Oh — my mom and dad. They're on my list too. I don't think either of them are the stalker."

Lydia giggled.

"But anyone else — particularly someone you've met recently — they're a potential suspect, yeah. So I'm going to need you both to think really hard and make me a list of all the people you've met or talked to over the past few weeks. Can you do that for me?"

Lydia nodded, her eyes glued to Sam's face. "Sure. I'll do it right away."

No, Lydia definitely wasn't immune to Sam's charm. Now, there was a thought that was frightening. Sam and Lydia. But their age difference was hardly much larger than the difference in Ellen and Sam's ages. It would be no more appropriate for Ellen to go out with Sam than it would be for Sam to go out with fifteen-year-old Lydia.

Ellen forced herself to look at Sam's feet, at the sneakers he was wearing. They were big and bold cross-trainers, with lightning bolts and stripes of black standing out against the white of the shoe. They were something Jamie would wear. They were unabashedly young looking.

And his jeans. She tried to picture Richard wearing jeans and a sport jacket to work, but she couldn't. Of course, Richard was a good ten years older than *she* was. He was from an even more formal upbringing.

"Why don't you get started on those lists," Sam told the kids. "It might help you remember people you've met if you work together — exactly like Captain Kirk and Commander Kang from 'The Day of the Dove,' " he added with a grin.

"Let's do it on the computer," Jamie said to Lydia.

"You just want me to type for you."

"You *like* to type. I know, you can pretend to be Lieutenant Uhura."

Lydia stood up, giving her brother a

thoroughly evil eye. "Lieutenant Uhura wasn't just some brainless space chick, you know. She was on track to becoming a captain."

"Last one to the computer's a brainless space chick," Jamie said.

Lydia snorted. "Oh, grow up."

But when Jamie stood up and made a move toward the door, Lydia bolted, beating him there. They disappeared down the hallway, both running full speed.

"Don't . . ." Ellen gave up and finished the last of her sentence in a regular voice, ". . . run in the house." She looked at Sam and rolled her eyes. "At least I can take comfort from the fact that they're not running with scissors in their hands."

Sam laughed as he stood up and closed the door to the sitting room. "I'll need a similar list from you."

"You just closed the door," Ellen said.

"Yeah, I did that on purpose. I wanted to talk for a minute in private."

"About?"

He smiled ruefully. "Nothing personal. This case — and your kids." He paused. "They're great, you know."

"Yes, I do know. What about them?"

Ellen knew what he was going to say before he even said it.

Sam's blue eyes were serious. "I think we need to be open to the possibility that Lydia or Jamie might be the stalker's target."

Ellen felt a flash of hot and then cold. She'd known he was going to say that; still, hearing the words spoken aloud made them frighteningly real.

He sat down on the couch, next to her, and for a moment she thought he was going to take her hand. For a moment she wanted him to. Desperately. But he didn't.

"I don't think that's necessarily true," he continued, "but it's smart to be ready for any possibility."

She looked up at him. "You don't think . . . ?" The phone rang. Ellen looked at it and then at Sam. "That's Bob's personal line. Have you set up the equipment to trace incoming calls yet?"

He shook his head. "That won't be installed until sometime tonight."

"I'm expecting my agent to call," Ellen said. But she didn't reach for the phone.

"Do you want me to answer it?"

She shook her head. "No." Drawing in a deep breath, she picked up the phone. "Hello?"

"He's back," the voice said. It was the caller. The stalker. The creep. Ellen looked sharply at Sam. "It's him," she said sound-lessly.

"Keep him talking," he mouthed silently. "Is there another phone in here?"

She shook her head no. "Who's back?" she asked the caller. "Who is this?"

Sam moved to her other side, sitting close, adjusting the telephone and leaning in so that he could hear too. Ellen could feel his leg pressed against hers from his hip all the way to his knee. She could feel his shoulder, too, and his hand around hers as together they held the phone between them. She closed her eyes, too well aware of his mouth only inches from hers. His breath smelled sweet. Coffee and mint. She remembered how delicious he had tasted.

"There's no escape — only surrender," the voice hissed into both of their ears. "Death is coming."

Ellen opened her eyes and found Sam gazing at her. "When?" she asked. "When is it coming?"

"Soon. They have told me. It must be soon."

"Who are 'they?'" Ellen asked as Sam nodded slightly, reassuringly, still looking into her eyes. She held his gaze as if it were a lifeline.

"They are watching." The voice tightened,

the words coming faster and closer together. "Always watching."

Ellen's own throat felt tight, and she wondered if her own fear could be heard in her voice. She could very well be talking to her executioner. Sam's fingers tightened around hers as if he were thinking the same thoughts. She closed her eyes, tipping her head slightly so that it rested against his. She needed the contact. She wanted to feel his warmth. "You said death is coming. How will death come?" Her voice sounded hoarse.

"I don't know. They will tell me when the time is right."

She opened her eyes to see that Sam's were closed. But as if he sensed her watching him, he opened his eyes too. The sudden brilliance of blue was startlingly beautiful. She was close enough to see that his eyes were blue and only blue. There were no flecks and streaks of green and gold, like Jamie's eyes. "Haven't they even given you a hint?" she asked the caller.

"All that is certain is the probe."

Shoot, not the probe. Ellen didn't want this freak talking about the probe. First came talk of the probe, then came the list of probe-able human body parts. He seemed really to enjoy running down that list and including all kinds of unpleasant euphemisms. She shivered slightly, and Sam gazed at her searchingly, concern in his eyes as he slipped his arm around her shoulders, holding her even closer. "We can hang up," he said soundlessly.

She shook her head, but she didn't pull away from him. "Did you send those pictures?" she asked the caller.

"I do their bidding." In the background she could hear the blare of a siren getting louder and then fading away.

"Look, it's a yes or no question. Did you or didn't you send me those creepy pictures?" Her voice rose sharply.

"Death and life," he said, almost chanting. "Death and life. One leads to the other."

"Yeah, life to death, and not the other way around." But Sam was shaking his head slightly, warningly. Ellen took a deep breath and tried to make her voice sound calm. "Why are you calling me?"

"Where do you want them to put the probe?"

"Lord, will you stop with the probe crap," Ellen said.

"Where do you want them to put the probe?"

Ellen lost it. "How about up your nose with a rubber hose, nutball?"

On the other end of the phone there was silence. A long, shocked silence. And then the foul language started. Again it was almost like a chant, a series of meaningless syllables that were strung together.

Sam reached across Ellen and with one finger cut the connection.

She dropped the receiver as if it were tainted, and didn't fight him as he wrapped her in his arms.

"I'm sorry," he murmured, kissing her hair as she buried her face in his shirt. "God, Ellen, I'm so sorry. Dammit, I wish we'd been hooked up to trace that call. I wish we'd gotten that on tape."

"I'm going to have to do that again." She closed her eyes tightly. As long as she kept her eyes closed, she could pretend that she wasn't sitting there with Sam's arms around her, with his fingers in her hair, his hands running down her back. "The next time he calls, I'm going to have to talk to him again so we can try to trace it, aren't I?"

"Yeah." Sam swore softly. "And all we'll probably find out is that he's calling from a public phone — which we already know."

Ellen opened her eyes. "We do?"

He nodded, looking down at her. "Didn't you hear the street noise? He was calling from some corner pay phone."

"Now that you mention it . . ."

The hard lines of Sam's face softened into a smile. "Up your nose with a rubber hose, huh?"

Ellen found herself smiling back at him — until he brushed her hair back from her face, his fingers gentle against her cheek.

Then, suddenly, she realized his mouth was no more than two inches away from hers. His smile faded, too, and his eyes seemed almost piercing in their intensity. And then the two inches became one, and one inch became none as she lifted her mouth to meet his in a kiss.

Lord, she'd missed him this past week.

He kissed her just as he had that very first time in the limo — possessively, hungrily, proprietarily. His kiss was thoroughly consuming, and Ellen let herself be swept away, leaving the unpleasantness of that phone call and all of the threats and dangers it implied far behind.

All that existed was Sam.

His mouth was so sweet, his lips so demanding, she couldn't pull back. She didn't want to. It wasn't until his hand swept up her body, cupping her breast through the cotton of her T-shirt, that reality intervened.

She pulled back and pushed herself off the couch, practically throwing herself to the other side of the room, well out of his reach.

"Lord," she said, holding on to the back of a chair for support. "Don't do that."

He stood up too. "Don't do what? Kiss you back when you kiss me? You're kidding, right?"

Dear God, *she'd* kissed him. *She* was the one who'd lifted her mouth that last fraction of an inch and kissed him. "I'm sorry."

"I'm not." He stepped toward her. "Ellen —"

She backed away. "Don't. Don't get too close."

"Why? Because you'll kiss me again? That sounds like incentive for me to get as close as I possibly can as often as I possibly can."

"Please," she said, keeping the chair between them. "I didn't mean for that to happen."

Frustration and desire burned in his eyes. "You may not have meant for it to happen, but it was the most honest interaction we've shared since we said good night a week ago Friday."

She flushed. "That was a mistake, what we did that night —"

He lowered his voice, and the effect was even more dangerous than if he'd raised it.

"The *hell* it was. It was perfect, and you know it."

"It was a mistake because I misjudged you," Ellen told him. "You weren't supposed to want more than one night."

The look in Sam's eyes was unreadable. "You know, you said you'd never done that kind of thing before — have a one-night stand with a stranger. But now I've really got to wonder."

Ellen was outraged, but her flare of temper didn't last. It was quickly doused by a flood of shame. He had every right to think ill of her. "I haven't," she whispered. "I wouldn't."

"So, what makes me different?" Sam's gaze was probing, searching her eyes, trying to read her mind. "What makes me eligible for only one night, even though I've made it clear I want more than that?"

"I'm not ready for . . . someone like you." Someone who would take her heart and run. She edged toward the door. "Please, let's not complicate things," she added.

"Ellen, I've got to be honest with you — things have been complicated beyond belief since you told me you didn't want to see me again. I don't know why you won't give us a chance. I see you and I still want you," he said, his husky voice nearly breaking with desire, "and I look into your eyes and I know you still want me. And I just can't figure this out."

"I didn't come to New York looking for a summer fling."

"You came looking for a change, though," he reminded her. "A temporary change of pace. You told me yourself you've been alone for four years. We could change that right now. We could be having a truly great summer if you would just relax and let it happen."

"I can't. We . . . we come from such different worlds." She was unwilling to tell him the whole truth — that she was terrified of falling in love with him, of leaving her heart behind in New York when she returned to Connecticut at the end of the summer. She didn't know how to have a light romance, a summer fling. She had never had a relationship where she'd held back, where she hadn't given all. Even during that single night she'd spent with Sam, she'd given away a little too much of her heart. She knew that now as she stood there gazing at him, wishing she were enough of a fool to throw her caution to the wind and herself into his arms.

But she was only a bit of a fool. She was smart enough to know that even if she were ready for a relationship again, she wasn't going to become involved with a too handsome, too young, too charismatic ladies' man who would probably pull a Richard and cheat on her further down the road — provided he stuck around long enough for there even to be a road. Add on top of that the fact that come September they'd live over a hundred miles apart . . .

No, mistakes were made to learn from, and Ellen was determined to learn from her failed marriage if it was the last thing she'd ever do.

Bob had mentioned introducing her to his stage manager, a nice, friendly, funny, thirty-something man who'd been widowed for nearly four years. He even lived in Connecticut, down in Westport, about midway between New York City and Ellen. Bob had mentioned him a week ago. He sounded perfect. So why hadn't Ellen done anything about it? Why hadn't she asked Bob to invite the man over for dinner?

She was looking into the neon blue eyes of the reason why.

Sam looked unhappy and subdued. He looked as if he were about to say something more, but instead he just shook his head. "I better go. I'm already late for a meeting at the precinct."

Ellen tried not to watch him walk away.
And failed.

NINE

Sam was sweating. He had every right to be hot. The casting agency was crowded, the current heat wave was sending the mercury up near one hundred degrees, and the building's wheezing old air-conditioning system was being pushed as far as it could go with no obvious effect.

But Sam's sweat was the cold, nasty kind. The kind that came from nerves and stress.

Outwardly, he knew he looked calm and relaxed. He knew he was good at throwing off an air of solid confidence. Inside, he was coming up with a huge list of all the awful things that could go wrong before they were back in the safety of Bob's house.

Compiled with the things that already *had* gone wrong that day, it was a load of anxiety worthy of the coldest of sweats.

Someone had followed them as he and Ellen and the kids had left the house. Sam had spotted the tail almost right away as they'd walked the few blocks over to the agency's office. But he'd never managed to get a clear look at the man's face. Even more frustrating was the fact that his backup team lost the guy.

Sam had wanted nothing more than to circle around behind the son of a bitch and catch him off guard, but he couldn't do it himself. And there was no way in hell he was going to leave Ellen and the kids alone. Still, his inability to act had frustrated him beyond reason. He wanted to catch this creep and make the glimmer of fear he could see in Ellen's eyes disappear for good.

She'd told him that their worlds were too different. Wasn't that the truth? His world was filled with scumbags like this one, scumbags who frequently tried to invade her world.

And then, of course, there was the tricky little matter of education. Her world was also an academic world. She spent her time bringing a higher level of learning to some of the brightest students in the country. She had more degrees hanging off the end of her name than everyone in Sam's family combined. She spent most of her time in the idyllic scholarly peace of a college campus.

Sam, on the other hand, lived in a world

where his job entailed tracking down a deranged killer who didn't even know how to spell the word that he specialized in — *death.* Of course, Sam wasn't that strong a speller himself, never had been. It hadn't bothered him before. But now he felt self-conscious about it — as if somehow that made him no better than the man he was after. God help him if he ever had to write Ellen a note. He was going to have to start carrying around a pocket dictionary.

Sam looked at his watch. They'd been there for nearly an hour, waiting for their turn in the audition room. Ellen sat with Lydia and Jamie on a row of chairs against the wall. They were quiet, reading something Lydia had called "sides" that looked like a two-page script.

The room they were waiting in was little more than a wide hallway. There were several doors off the hallway, all of which remained shut, opening and closing only under the power of a stout woman with a clipboard and a piercing voice. The doors opened, the woman used her megaphone voice to bleat out a name, an actor went in, and the doors shut — sometimes not even for a full minute. Then the doors opened again, the actor was expelled, another name bleated, and another, different actor went in.

Except there wasn't really that big a difference between the first actor and the second. Everyone in this room — with the exception of Sam, the lady with the clipboard, and several stage mothers — was either a thirty-something light-haired woman, a freckle-faced boy, or an on-the-verge-of-beautiful young teenage girl.

Farther down the hallway a group of balding, overweight men wearing business suits and eyeglasses were all sitting or standing outside of another closed door.

It was weird, but it was good. Unless the stalker was a woman, a kid, a young girl, or a balding, overweight, business-suited man, Sam would have no problem spotting him the moment he appeared.

"What do you think of your first cattle call?"

Sam turned around to see Ellen standing behind him, close but not too close. He had a feeling she wasn't going to get too close ever again. He'd barely slept at all last night, aware that she was lying in her bed, in a room up on the next floor, so close and yet so far away.

"This actually would be pretty amusing," Sam said, "if I didn't have other things to think about." He gestured to the door. "What goes on in there that they have to close the door so tightly?"

Ellen smiled. "Well, for one thing, there's probably a window air conditioner that's keeping the room nice and cool, because the client's in there. He or she is paying the casting agency big bucks to parade a bunch of quality talent — that's us — in front of them. We go in, and the clients — sometimes there's a group of them — are sitting behind a table. There's a video camera set up, and we look into the camera, give our name, our agent, and whatever other information they ask us to give. Sometimes they say 'Thank you,' and we leave without even reading the sides. Sometimes they have us read the lines three or four times. Sometimes they like what we do and they laugh — if it's supposed to be funny, that's really good. But sometimes they barely even glance up, and spend the entire time we're there talking to someone on their cell phone."

Sam scanned the crowd, noting the new people who arrived, watching them sign in at the different tables around the room. "Man, that sounds awful."

Ellen looked back at Lydia and Jamie, still sitting in the folding chairs against the wall. "Yeah. It's really an interesting business.

The amount of rejection you face is huge. I'm kind of awed that both my kids have stuck with it for so long."

In between the careful, calculated sweeps Sam made of the room, searching for anyone different, anyone who looked out of place, he glanced at her face.

"I wanted to tell you that I've crossed Richard off my list of suspects," Sam said quietly.

Ellen's dark eyes widened in surprise. "Richard? Was a suspect?"

Sam slipped his hands in the pockets of his jeans as he leaned against one of the round support pillars that dotted the room. He met her eyes only briefly before he focused a portion of his attention on a man who had just gotten off the elevator. But the man was accompanying a ten-year-old freckle-faced boy. Sam watched as they went to one of the tables and signed in.

"It's standard procedure," he told her, "based on the fact that most violent crimes are committed by someone who was close to the victim. In cases like this it would be crazy not to check out the ex-husband."

"And Richard checks out okay?"

Sam nodded. "He's been in San Francisco since the beginning of June."

"I could have told you that."

"We verified with the San Francisco police that he really is in California."

She was watching him closely, and when she spoke, her words surprised him. "Are you still upset by what happened before?"

At first he didn't understand what she was referring to. Then he realized she had to be talking about the way they'd been followed and the clumsy attempt — and failure — to apprehend the stalker. He'd been *really* upset, but he hadn't thought anyone had known. He'd purposely played it super cool.

She looked away, as if aware she'd somehow given away too much. If she'd been watching him closely enough to know that he was, indeed, quite upset . . .

"Ellen, do you like me?"

His question surprised her and she glanced up at him. He could see the uncertainty in her eyes as she hesitated to answer him.

He made another sweep around the room before he glanced back at her. "It's not a trick question. I think you like me, and I just wanted to know if I was right or not."

Ellen nodded, giving him a ghost of one of her usual ebullient smiles. "Yes, I like you." She looked as if she were going to add something else, but then she stopped, a slight flush tingeing her cheeks.

Sam waited until she looked up at him again, and then he said, "I like you, too, you know. This thing between us — it's more than just sex. I wanted to make sure you knew that."

"Are you telling me that you want to be . . . friends?"

"I think maybe what I'm telling you is that we *are* friends already. Despite the fact that you'd rather not be."

Ever since he'd kissed Ellen the day before and she'd had a near heart attack, he'd realized he was pushing too hard, hoping for too much. And as much as he wanted to leap headlong into a sexual relationship with this woman, that wasn't all that he wanted. He wanted to be with her. And he'd achieved that. He was living in her house, which provided a lot of opportunities to be with her. And given a little bit of time, he would build on their friendship — this strong sense of *like* that he knew was between them. And once that happened, it was only a matter of more time before the nearly overpowering attraction they felt became impossible to ignore.

"I'm not going anywhere," he told her quietly. "That's something else I wanted to make sure you understood."

"Ellen Layne!" called the woman with the clipboard.

Ellen didn't move.

"That's you," Sam reminded her. "Break a leg."

"Ellen Layne?" the woman bleated again, and Ellen turned away, heading for the door.

She glanced at him over her shoulder just before the door closed, and Sam could see her emotions swirling in the depths of her eyes.

His own feelings were so strong, so over-powering, he had to hold on to the support pole for a moment to maintain his balance. Damn, this infatuation was the most power-ful he'd ever felt.

Maybe because it was more than mere infatuation . . .

Sam tried to push that thought out of his mind, not wanting to acknowledge it, not wanting to give it more definite shape and meaning. He thought about what T.S. had told him instead. Maybe T.S. was right. Maybe the crush Sam had on Ellen was spinning out of control due to her rejection. She didn't want him, so of course he wanted her even more than ever.

He kept his gaze moving, feeling the familiar knot of anxiety in his stomach as a scruffily dressed man came into the room.

He relaxed slightly as he saw the messenger's envelope the man was carrying. Still, he watched the man until he passed out of sight.

The door opened and Ellen came out, talking with the woman who carried the clipboard, smiling and laughing.

Sam's chest felt as if it were expanding. He smiled almost involuntarily and felt a burst of that same happiness, that *joy,* he'd felt in the limo, this time merely at the sight of her.

And he recognized the symptoms even though he'd never truly experienced them before.

He was falling in love with Ellen Layne.

The security guards and police officers were nearly as numerous as the party guests.

Ellen glanced around the private dining room at the Cafe Allessandra, a tiny Italian place on Restaurant Row, aware of Sam standing on the other side of the room. He wasn't exactly watching her, but she knew, just as she was aware of every move he made, that he was equally aware of her.

He wasn't going to let her forget about that night of passion they'd shared. *That* was what he'd really meant to say the day before at the audition.

She'd managed to avoid him successfully all last night and then all that day, but when Bob had called to announce that his contract dispute with the network had been settled, that he was throwing an impromptu dinner for his staff, Ellen had leapt at his invitation to join him. She hadn't been able to stand the thought of staying home alone with Sam, with only Jamie and Lydia to chaperone. Not only that, but it was, as Bob put it, the perfect time for Ellen to meet his stage manager, Leonard Jennison. Poor Bob had no idea how totally wrong he was.

Still, Ellen was here, despite Sam's objections.

But Bob had reassured him as to the safety. Since his contract was settled, he'd told the studio about the death threats, and they had sent six of their security guards to the shindig as extra protection. With Sam and Hyunh along, that made eight law enforcement officials to the twenty partygoers. All of the exits were carefully guarded. Even Sam had to agree that they were as safe as they could possibly be.

Bob made a point of seating Ellen next to Leonard Jennison at the dinner table, and she could feel Sam watching, sizing Jennison up, taking in Bob's attempts at playing Cupid.

She wasn't surprised when Sam intercepted her on her way to the ladies' room.

"He's too old for you," he said without even saying hello.

Ellen didn't bother to pretend that she didn't know what he was talking about. "If you want to know the truth, he's a year younger than me," she told him.

"I was speaking figuratively," he said. "In terms of attitude. He *acts* old. Too old for you."

"He's a nice guy."

"I'm nicer." Sam pushed open the door to the ladies' room and looked quickly inside, checking for lurking stalkers. It was empty.

Ellen had to laugh. "I'm not so sure about that. I'm betting Leonard's never even *touched* the ladies' room door in his entire life, let alone opened it."

"Since when is that the definition of nice?" Sam asked. "It's just a room." He opened the door and stepped inside, taking her hand and pulling her in with him. "I can even go inside, and I'm *still* nicer."

"You're more entertaining, that's for sure."

"Well, okay." Sam smiled at her. "That's a start."

He was certainly nicer to look at too.

"You shouldn't be in here," Ellen said.

He leaned against the hand dryer. "Just think of yourself as being extremely safe."

"Safe?" Ellen looked at him pointedly, her gaze traveling slowly down his body, taking in his loosened tie and somewhat wrinkled white shirt, his tweed sport coat, the faded blue jeans that covered his long, muscular legs, his glaringly decorated sneakers. By the time she looked up into his face, that dimple had appeared in his cheek, and his eyes were brimming with both amusement and heat. "I don't think 'safe' is a word I'd ever use in context with you," she added. "Because after you're done keeping me safe from all of the bad guys, who's going to keep me safe from *you?*"

Something changed in his eyes at that. "You don't have to be kept safe from me," he said quietly. "I swear to you, Ellen, I'm playing totally by your rules. You want me? I'm here. You don't? I keep my distance. It's that simple. It's your call."

Her mouth was suddenly dry, and she had to moisten her lips. Her voice trembled. "Well, then, who's going to keep me safe from myself? Because I *do* want you."

He pushed himself up and off the hand dryer, but Ellen held up her hand as if making sure he stayed at least an arm's length away. "But even more than I want you, I *don't* want to risk becoming involved with you." She took a deep breath. "I'm finding when it comes to you, it's hard for me to resist the temptation."

"Why is it such a risk for you to be involved with me?" Sam's voice was low, imploring. His eyes held her hypnotizingly in place. "Come on, Ellen. Help me to understand where you're coming from."

The bathroom door swung open, and Ellen nearly jumped out of her skin. It was Hyunh and she stopped short when she saw Sam. "Oops. Am I interrupting?"

Ellen forced a smile. "No, actually, Sam was just leaving. He was getting a little *too* in touch with his feminine side."

No one laughed.

Hyunh looked from Ellen to Sam, and Ellen knew the older woman didn't miss the intensity of Sam's gaze or the serious set to his mouth as he said, "This conversation will be continued."

"Everything okay?" Hyunh asked as the door closed behind Sam.

Ellen made herself smile again. "Everything's . . . great."

Hyunh lifted an eyebrow. "We had an old saying back in Saigon. It translates roughly into something like 'Liar, liar, pants on fire.' "

Ellen laughed. And then, to her horror, her eyes filled with tears.

"Oh, boy," Hyunh said sympathetically. "You got it bad for this one, huh?"

Ellen nodded. Yes. She had it bad. For Sam.

Sam saw Tran Minh Hyunh come out of the corridor that led to the ladies' room. The Vietnamese woman leaned over next to Bob and spoke softly in his ear. They both looked up, directly at him, and then Hyunh headed back toward the ladies' room.

Bob stood and sauntered around the table toward Sam. "Me and you. Right now," he said, his usual friendly warmth decidedly absent. "Private meeting in the men's room."

Sam moved down the hall, several steps behind Bob. Ellen still hadn't come out of the ladies' room, and he hesitated outside that door. "Is Ellen all right?"

Bob turned to face him. "You tell me. She was really upset about something, and Hyunh took her home."

"What?" Sam pushed open the ladies' room door, receiving a startled squeak from a gray-haired woman putting on lipstick in front of the mirror. He went inside anyway and quickly pushed the half-open doors to the stalls. Ellen was definitely not there. "Where the hell is she?"

"Sorry, Verna," Bob called to the gray-haired woman as he pulled Sam not too gently out of the room. "They went out the back door."

Sam shook off Bob's grip, moving quickly toward the back exit. It was supposed to have been left locked. "I have to go after her."

But Bob blocked his path, suddenly looking more like an ex-Marine than a popular late night talk show host. "She's fine. She's safe. Hyunh's with her."

But Sam wasn't buying that. "Man, you don't understand." His heart was pounding and he couldn't keep the fear from creeping into his voice. "I listened to this guy talk to Ellen on the phone. This is one crazy mother—"

Bob took a slender cell phone from his jacket pocket and flipped it open. He pressed a speed dial number and waited a few seconds. "Hi, it's me," he said into the phone. "Are you safe?"

He held out the phone to Sam.

"We're in the limo," Hyunh's voice said through the miniature telephone. "We're halfway home. I've already called the house. Pete will come out to meet us while Barney stays in the house with the kids. We'll call you when we're safely inside."

"Look," Sam said, trying hard to stay in control. "Just tell the driver to turn around and come back and pick me up. Please."

"I'm with Ellen," Hyunh said. "I'm counting on you to stick close to Bob. I'll call when we're safely inside the house."

The connection was cut, and there was nothing for Sam to do but hand the telephone back to Bob. He wanted to fling the damn thing against the wall, but he didn't.

Bob pushed open the men's room door, gesturing for Sam to go ahead of him inside the blue-tiled room. Sam caught sight of himself in the mirrors above the sinks, and he knew that everything he was feeling, all the frustration and fear and despair, was written clearly on his face.

"So, what exactly did you do to Ellen?" the older man asked. "Or maybe I should be asking what *she* did to *you?*"

Sam turned on the water in one of the sinks and, pushing up his sleeves, let it run on his wrists, trying to cool himself down. "It was mutual. Or so I thought."

"I was going to bring you in here and tell you if you so much as looked at her the wrong way, I was going to kick your ass from here to Outer Mongolia." Bob examined his teeth in the mirror. "But you look like your ass has already been kicked."

Sam dried his hands on a paper towel and threw it with unerring accuracy into the garbage can across the room. "I have to get back to your house."

"Hyunh thought that Ellen needed some time without you hanging around."

Sam's temper flared. "What Ellen wants is for me not to hang around for the entire rest of her life. There'll be plenty of time for that after this case is over. Until then, I'm going to make damn sure she's safe."

Bob placed himself squarely between Sam and the door. "You know, if I were you, I'd try to figure out why she's running so scared. A little finesse might work a whole lot better than repeatedly trying to force your perspective on her. I don't know how much she's told you about her divorce —"

"I know about Richard." Sam gestured toward the door. "Do you mind letting me pass?"

"Do you know that she *had* to marry him?"

That stopped Sam. "No. I didn't. You mean . . . ?"

"He got her pregnant. He was older than she was — older than me, in fact, although I'm only eight years older than Ellen, so that's not saying much. But he was . . . how shall I put this politely? A slimeball. Oh, he was successful and handsome and well educated, but when I met him I knew he was the kind of guy you couldn't trust any farther than you could throw. I *begged* Ellen not to marry him."

"But she did."

"She couldn't see past the designer haircut and the capped teeth." Bob leaned back against the door. "She figured they were going to get married after she graduated from college anyway — this just pushed everything up a few years."

"At least he did the right thing by her," Sam pointed out.

Bob snorted. "What? Marry the girl he got pregnant, and continue sleeping with any other women stupid enough to glance in his direction?"

Sam was silent.

"She needs to know that this time around she's making her own decisions. She needs to feel that this time she's got a choice."

"Whoa," Sam said. "Wait a minute here. *This* time around?"

Bob got a little bit taller. "Your intentions are honorable, aren't they, Schaefer?"

Sam stood his ground. "My intentions are to keep this thing we've got from dying before it has a chance to get off the ground. My intentions are to see where this thing can go." Intentions. Honorable. God. Bob made it sound as if he expected Sam to *marry* Ellen.

Except, oddly enough, the idea didn't make his blood run as cold as it had when he'd thought about the M-word in the past. Instead it brought to mind images of waking up with Ellen beside him in bed — guaranteed. It brought to mind images of them both helpless and giddy with laughter, clinging together. It brought to mind images of Ellen talking to him long into the night, warmth and a beautiful softness in her exquisite eyes as she leaned close to kiss him.

But who was he kidding? Ellen didn't want to talk to him, let alone marry him.

And then Sam stopped thinking, because from out in the restaurant came the sounds of a muffled explosion and shattering glass and the hubbub of raised, excited voices.

Sam pushed past Bob and threw open the door. He could smell the pungent odor of smoke as he ran down the corridor, Bob on his heels. The private dining room was thick with it, and he could see flames dancing up along the heavy curtains that lined the windows. People were pushing past him, coughing and choking, trying to get to the exit.

Sam turned back to Bob. "Get these people to the back door," he shouted over the confusion. "Try to get a head count!"

Bob nodded, and Sam turned back to the room, covering his face with the tail of his shirt. The window had been broken, and something, some kind of smoke bomb perhaps, had been thrown into the room. But a smoke bomb wouldn't account for the flames.

As far as he could see, no one had been hurt.

Yet.

He looked up at the ceiling. Why hadn't the sprinkler system kicked on?

The smoke was chokingly thick, swirling around him, making it hard to tell which direction was up. A woman was staggering nearby, coughing and hacking. Sam grabbed the woman's arm, pulling her toward the door. God, if there was anyone else in here . . .

He felt his way back down the corridor, pushing the woman ahead of him. Somewhere in the building a fire alarm had been pulled, and he could hear its urgent, relentlessly shrill ringing. He stumbled out of the back door after the woman he was helping, the two of them gasping and coughing, pulling in long, deep breaths of fresh air.

Sam had never thought of the air in a New York City back alley as fresh before, but compared to the smoke, it was glorious.

"You all right?" Bob asked him.

Sam leaned over, wracked with coughing. His lungs felt lined with soot and he felt dizzy from lack of oxygen. "Yeah," he gasped, trying to straighten up, his voice raspy and his throat raw and sore. "Head count?"

"Short one," Bob said tersely. "As far as I can tell, it's Verna. One of my secretaries."

Sam swore.

"Fire trucks're on their way," Bob reported, "but it'll be a good five minutes before they get here. I'm going in to look for her."

"No," Sam said. "I'll go in, with one of the guards."

"Which one?" Bob asked dryly. "The one who passed out or the one who's sitting on the curb crying?"

Sam swore again as Bob pushed past him, heading for the door. Thick gray smoke was streaming out, but that didn't slow him down. Sam had to run to keep up.

"Stay low," he ordered Bob hoarsely. "We'll make a sweep of the room, meet at the window, and use a couple of chairs to break the rest of the glass. There's only about a six-foot drop to the street. If we find her, we can get her out that way."

Bob nodded. "You go left, I'll go right."

The smoke made it impossible to see, impossible to breathe. And still the sprinklers hadn't switched on. If Verna was in the room, she was surely on the floor, unconscious. Sam could hear the flames crackling, feel the heat, see the hellish glow of the fire. His eyes burned and teared and he dropped to the carpeting, feeling his way, searching for the prone body of Bob's secretary. Please God, let him find her . . .

He bumped into a chair that had been pushed onto its side next to the dining table. He knew the window was just on the other side of the table. He could throw a chair or two through it, maybe draw some of this smoke out of the room.

Sam pulled himself up to climb over the table and —

A man appeared as if conjured up out of the smoke and flames, like the devil himself. Sam jumped back, startled, but then realized it was a fireman, dressed in a gas mask and raincoat, with a hard, protective hat on his head.

Sam kept his shirt over his face, raising

his voice to be heard over the roar of the fire. "There's still someone in here," he shouted.

The fireman nodded and picked up a chair. He was clearly thinking along the same lines as Sam — break the window. But it was funny he didn't have an ax and —

He didn't have time to finish that thought before the fireman lifted the chair above his head and sent it crashing down on top of Sam. There was only enough time to roll with the blow, but it was enough to keep the heavy wood from crushing his skull. Still, the chair connected with his shoulder, the force smashed him down onto the table, knocking the wind from his lungs as the wood splintered. Sam tried to roll away, using his arms to block the man's next swing, trying in vain to reach for his gun, but unable both to arm himself and to ward off the frenzied attack as the smoke from the fire filled his lungs, choking him.

He pushed himself back, kicking hard with his feet and legs, kicking up. He felt his foot connect with something soft — the man's face or neck — but the savage blows kept coming, raining down on his head and chest and shoulders. He felt the jagged edge of the wood tear through his sleeve, cutting his arm. The pain only slightly penetrated the ever narrowing tunnel of darkness that was surrounding him as his lungs ached for air.

This man wanted him dead, and it was entirely possible that he was going to succeed.

Sam had been wrong about a lot of things, but the most obvious was that he'd been mistaken about the stalker. This guy wasn't after Ellen. He was after Bob. In the smoke and the darkness, this man thought that Sam was Bob.

Sam had made a mistake with Ellen too. He'd spent the past two evenings under the same roof and he hadn't gone to her room either night and demanded they talk. He hadn't fallen down on his knees and confessed his feelings for her.

Maybe she would've laughed in his face. But maybe she wouldn't have.

Maybe she would've kissed him. Maybe she would've admitted that she felt something for him too. Maybe.

Dammit, he wasn't going to die without knowing. With a strength he didn't know he had, Sam rolled over, exposing the back of his head to the sharp wood of the broken chair. The blow nearly took the last of his consciousness, but somehow he managed to turn, gun drawn, and face his attacker. He fired, but the man was gone, vanished into the smoke.

Sam rolled across the table, desperate for air. He could see the flames reflecting off the window, and he pushed himself harder, propelling himself through the air, tucking his head under and diving through the already broken glass.

He hit the sidewalk hard, pain ripping through his battered body. And then there was only black.

Ten

Ellen was in the kitchen when Bob and Sam came home.

She cursed softly at her bad timing. She'd been planning to be upstairs, safely behind her closed bedroom door. She'd been planning not to have to see Sam until the next evening at the earliest.

She briefly considered abandoning the kettle of water that was heating on the stove and the mug with the herbal tea bag she was holding in her hands, and dashing for the stairs.

But she didn't move quickly enough, and the back door opened.

"You sure you're all right?" Bob asked, turning to look behind him.

"I need a shower." Sam's voice sounded raspy and hoarse.

"You and me both," Bob agreed.

Ellen dropped the mug she was holding onto the floor, where it bounced before spinning and coming to a rest on its side.

Both men looked as if they'd recently taken jobs as chimney sweeps. Streaks of soot and dirt covered their clothes and faces and hands. And Sam . . . Sam had an angry welt across his left cheekbone and a cut at the corner of his mouth, along with bright stains of blood on his shirt and in his hair. *Blood.*

"Hey, babe," he said, smiling crookedly, painfully at Ellen. "I know I'm risking being lambasted by saying that, but as you can see, I've already had my beating tonight, thanks."

He was trying to be funny, but Ellen didn't laugh. She crossed her arms, holding on to herself tightly to keep from rushing toward him.

"What happened?" she asked, looking to Bob for a real explanation.

But Sam answered. "Our crazy stalker tried to burn down the Cafe Allessandra. I had a little run-in with him. I think he thought I was Bob."

Bob?

"We were probably wrong," Bob admitted. "This guy's probably been after me this whole time. It would've been easy, in the smoke, to think Schaefer was me. We both went back into the room together. But there was no way this guy could've mistaken Sam for *you*. The only part we haven't quite figured out is the obscene phone calls."

"I've been thinking about that. It's possible this guy doesn't want to talk to you, Bob. He just wants to kill you. He *did* say, 'He's back,' right after you returned from Boston," Sam pointed out.

"Wait a minute," Ellen interrupted. "What happened *tonight?* Start from the beginning."

Sam pulled out one of the kitchen chairs and painfully lowered himself into it. "Someone — probably our stalker — threw a smoke bomb through the window of the back dining room. Then someone — probably the same man — came in and, in the confusion, lit the curtains and some gasoline-soaked rags on fire, heating up the place. Someone previously — and it's not a long stretch to assume we're talking about the same guy — disconnected the restaurant's sprinkler system."

"And then, after Sam and I went back to search for Verna Horton, who was missing, someone wearing a gas mask and fireman's getup tried to bludgeon Sam to death with a wooden chair," Bob added. "I, of course, was no help during this, because I had found Verna about three steps away from the door and had taken her out the back. By then the fire department had arrived, and they wouldn't let me back inside to help Sam.

"I went around to the front of the restaurant, where the window was, because that's where Sam told me he'd meet me, but before I even got there, I saw him come flying out of the window like Batman."

"Batman would've landed on his feet," Sam told Bob.

"After the paramedics revived him —"

Ellen couldn't hold it in any longer. "*Revived* him? My God!"

". . . we took a little side trip to the hospital, where Sam toured the X-ray department —"

"Nothing's broken," Sam volunteered. "Just bruised."

"Those restaurant chairs are heavy," Bob said. "If this guy had swung it hard enough and connected with Sam's head . . . I could damn well be coming home alone right now."

Ellen drew in a sharp breath. Sam glanced up at her, but he didn't deny what Bob had said. He could have been killed.

"I was just glad you weren't there, Ellen," Sam said quietly, his eyes so somber.

Ellen couldn't help herself. She took a

step toward Sam, and then another step.

He pushed himself up and out of that chair, holding his arms open for her.

She held him as tightly as she dared, uncaring of the grime and soot that stained his clothes.

"This looks like my cue to leave," Bob said. "See you kids in the morning."

She could hear his footsteps fading away down the hall. She could hear Sam's heart pounding in his chest. It sounded so strong, so powerful. But while she was sitting at home, reading a book, that heart had very nearly stopped beating.

"I want to be with you tonight," he said softly.

Ellen's voice shook. "You should be in the hospital."

She lifted her head to look up at him, and she could see exhaustion in his face. Still, somehow he managed to smile.

"Yeah," he admitted. "I probably should be. But I wanted to be here more." He pushed her hair back from her face, and his smile faded away, leaving behind only lines of pain at the corners of his mouth and a soft vulnerability in his eyes. "There's something about almost dying that makes you want to be near the people you love," he whispered.

Ellen couldn't breathe. He didn't mean that. He couldn't have meant that. He was exaggerating. He was simply using this emotion-fraught situation to secure himself a place in her bed.

But Ellen didn't care about his motivation or his exaggerations. She only knew that what he wanted, she wanted too. She had no choice.

"Come on," she said. "I'll help you get cleaned up."

He tried not to lean on her as she helped him into the elevator, but she knew that every step he took hurt. He met her eyes after she pushed the button for the third floor — after he realized that she was taking him to her room.

"Amazing," Sam said. "I feel better already."

The human body had a truly remarkable resilience. Sam had a bruise on his shoulder that had already started turning rainbow shades when he'd had it X-rayed at the hospital. He'd come damn close to death from suffocation, and he'd had a blow to the head that had made him see stars and still made him feel a little dizzy. He wasn't completely sure that there weren't stray pieces of glass in his backside, he was dead tired, and he couldn't remember the last time so many parts of his body had hurt or stung or ached.

Except for one part of his body. One part of his body didn't hurt at all. And it was that part of his body — his heart — that was beating in triple time as Ellen led him out of the elevator and down the hall to her bedroom.

She locked the door behind them. Sam loved the sound of that bolt sliding home. It promised other, softer, far more intimate sounds.

"This room has a Jacuzzi in the bathroom," Ellen told him. "Do you want me to run you a bath?"

"Is it big enough for two?"

She led him to the bathroom door. It was. It was enormous. The bathroom with its separate shower stall and double sinks was almost larger than his entire studio apartment.

"Will you join me?" he asked softly.

She gently disengaged herself from his grasp and began running warm water into the gleaming tub. She looked incredibly good, dressed in a pair of baggy sweatshorts and a tank top with a row of tiny buttons down the front. Her long, gracefully shaped legs were bare, as were her feet. She had red nail polish on her toes, and her skin seemed to glisten in the soft light.

"Please?" he added, his heart in his throat.

She looked up at him and smiled crookedly. "You know that I will. Do you really think I'd bring you in here, lock the door, and then *not* get naked with you?"

"With you, I don't know," he admitted.

"You just have to promise to tell me if you're in pain."

"I'm in pain." He smiled. "But it has nothing to do with getting beat up."

She dried her hands and crossed toward him. "Just do me a favor? What you said before? Downstairs? Don't say it again."

Love. He'd used the dreaded L-word. "I'm sorry if I scared you. I scared myself too. But . . . it's true."

"Truth can be so difficult to measure."

"Stop quoting cryptic Chinese cookie fortunes," he told her, "and kiss me."

She came willingly into his arms. Her mouth was so gentle, her lips so sweet.

Sam had never been quite so glad to be alive.

"Let's get you out of these clothes," she murmured, her fingers unbuttoning the tattered remains of his shirt.

He winced as he tried to push his shirt off his bruised shoulder, then gave up trying and just let Ellen do it.

She gasped as she saw the purple and brown of his skin. "Oh, Sam."

It was worth it. Every last bump and bruise and welt was worth it — just to know that she cared. "It looks worse than it really is," he lied.

"That must hurt so badly."

"I'm fine."

She gave him a long look and he knew she wasn't fooled. But she didn't say anything. She just knelt down and untied his sneakers, then supported him while he kicked them off.

She glanced briefly up into his eyes as she unfastened the buckle of his belt. There was no doubt that she'd noticed his arousal. He pulled her closer, lifting her mouth to his for a long, searing kiss as he pressed the palm of her hand against the hard bulge in his pants. He heard her moan, felt her fingers curl around him.

Oh, yes, he was *very* glad to be alive. "Told you I was feeling fine," he murmured.

He fumbled with the tiny buttons on her top until he gave up and just pulled it over her head, with her help. Her bra followed just as easily, and he staggered at the incredible sensation of her full breasts pressed against his chest as she kissed him again. He hooked his fingers in both her shorts and her panties, sweeping them down her smooth legs in one swift motion. And then she was naked.

And embarrassed. He could see it in her eyes and on her face as he pulled back to look at her, and he didn't know why. She was beautiful — all soft curves and smooth skin and sweet female flesh.

"No fair," she said, trying to hide the blush that tinged her cheeks. "You still have your pants on."

"We can change that in a second." He skimmed his pants down his legs and stepped gingerly out of them. His shorts were a little more difficult to get rid of, but with Ellen's help, he finally succeeded.

She went into the tub then, slipping under the cover of the water. Sam stepped in more slowly, gingerly lowering himself down. He had about a thousand scrapes on his arms, shoulders, and back that he knew would sting really badly.

But it barely hurt at all when Ellen smiled at him. She rubbed her hands with a bar of soap and, starting with his fingers, began to wash him with her hands.

It felt decadently good as her hands traveled up his arms. She was so gentle and careful of his bruises, yet at the same time, she succeeded in washing him clean. And turning him totally on.

He used his own hands to quickly wash his face, wincing as the soap stung the scrape on his cheek. He dunked his head back, rinsing his hair. When he came back up, he used his hands to squeeze the water from his hair and his face.

Ellen straddled his thighs so that she could gently wash his chest and shoulders. "You've got some bruises along your ribs too. You're going to be sore tomorrow."

She leaned forward to kiss him and he moved her hips forward so that she was pressed against the length of him. It was a dangerous thing to do. One thrust of his hips would send him deeply inside of her. And without birth control or protection, that would be sheer insanity.

But sheer insanity had never been so tempting before.

"I'm going to be better than fine — especially if I can wake up in your bed, next to you." He moved to kiss her again, but she pulled back.

"Oops," she said. "You don't know. Of course you don't know — I didn't tell you."

He tried to pull her back to him, burying his face in the cool, wet softness of her breasts, not completely paying attention. "Didn't tell me what?"

"I got cast in a commercial. I have to be at the studio tomorrow at six A.M."

He sat very still, her words finally penetrating. "Six A.M. in the *morning?*"

Ellen smiled. "That's generally what A.M. means."

Sam closed his eyes. "Man, that sucks." He opened his eyes. "I mean, God, it's great that you got the job, babe, but, wow. Six A.M." It already was long after midnight. He was going to be hurting big time tomorrow if he had to be somewhere at six.

"You can wake up in my bed," Ellen told him, "but I won't be next to you."

"Yes, you will. Because I'm going to get up and go with you."

She moved against him, so agonizingly tempting, he had to clench his teeth to keep from groaning aloud. He had to find a condom. Now. Right now.

"You're so sweet," she whispered, taking his earlobe between her teeth. "I guess I won't yell at you for calling me babe."

"No, did I really?"

She was poised over him, driving him slowly insane, testing the edge of his control. "You most certainly did," she told him as he ignored the pain in his shoulder and reached for his pants and the condom in his wallet, pulling Ellen out of the water with him as he covered himself.

"God," he said, glancing up and smiling into her gorgeous brown eyes. "Sorry, babe."

She dissolved into laughter, and he felt it again — that incredible sense of joy and happiness he'd felt the last time they'd made love. It wasn't going to get any better than this.

But when he lowered them both back down into the water, and she shifted her hips, pushing herself down on top of him, it *did* get better.

Sam kissed her, afraid if he didn't occupy his mouth he'd try to tell her the way she made him feel.

He loved her.

It was almost absurd. He was always the one backing away from the L-word, running for cover from the threat of the C-word — commitment. Yet somehow he'd managed to fall for a woman who needed him to damn near die before she could admit that she cared even the least little bit about him.

He wanted to shout that he loved her, but he didn't dare.

Still, she'd seemed to be okay with the idea that he would spend what little remained of the night in her bed. That was a good thing, wasn't it? Wasn't it?

God, he was scared to death. He was terrified of the emotions he was feeling, and terrified that *she'd* be terrified of the way he felt, too, if she found out just how deeply he loved her. It was one giant terrorfest.

Not only that, but he was afraid he was going to wake up tomorrow and the intensity of his emotions would be totally gone. At the same time, he was also afraid he was going to wake up tomorrow and all of his feelings would still be there, that he'd still love her. He was afraid she didn't see him as more than a short, hot fling. He was afraid she was going to break his heart, the way he'd broken dozens of hearts before. Casually. Callously. Barely even aware of the damage done.

He was afraid to talk to her, afraid to find out that she actually did find him beneath her because he hadn't gone to college. He was afraid even to think about it.

The only thing he wasn't afraid of was making love to Ellen. He knew without a doubt that it was the only time he truly had power over her. When he made love to her, she was his, completely.

He drove himself more deeply inside of her, again and again, setting a rhythm he knew she loved, and she clung to him, her head thrown back, her full breasts taut with her arousal. He felt the beginnings of her release, and it pushed him over the edge. His own release was hot and fierce, a scorching fireball of sensation that made him cry out her name, leaving him dizzy and near delirious in its aftermath.

He couldn't keep from laughing. It seemed impossible that he could feel so incredibly, mind-blowingly good after the hell of the past evening.

Ellen sighed, her face pressed against his neck. "Hold me," she breathed. "My muscles have turned to mush, and if you let me go, I'll be just another Jacuzzi drowning statistic."

"I won't ever let you go," Sam whispered, wishing with all of his heart that she would let him make his words be true.

She was silent then, as if she, too, caught his underlying meaning. She drew in another deep breath, and it seemed to catch, as if on a sob.

Sam tried to see her face, but she kept it turned away from him. "Ellen, are you all right?" He couldn't keep anxiety from creeping into his voice. "I didn't hurt you, did I?"

"No, I just . . . I . . ." She took a deep breath, lifting her head to give him a rather forced-looking smile. "That was really . . . wonderful, and it just made me . . . I don't know . . . a little sad." She rolled her eyes. "I get silly sometimes."

He kissed her, wishing he could read her mind. "Why did it make you sad?"

Her smile was wistful. "It was so perfect. Nothing can really be that perfect."

"You want to make a bet? Give me a few minutes and we can do perfect all over again." He nuzzled her neck.

She laughed in disbelief, swatting gently at him. "Are you kidding? I bet you can't even stand up by yourself."

"Do we have to do it standing up? I was actually thinking that making love to you in a bed would be something of a novelty."

She laughed again. God, he loved the sound of her laughter. "Well, let's see," she said. "We've done the limo. And the Jacuzzi. I have to admit that I've always wanted to have wild sex in an elevator. . . ."

Sam closed his eyes. "I'm never going to be able to ride in an elevator with you ever again without thinking about that."

"And then there's the rooftop patio, under the stars. I've never made love there. Or, ooh, I know. The kitchen table."

It was his turn to laugh. "What?"

"Yeah. It's *very* sexy. I've seen it in the

movies all the time. Pounding, steamy sex complete with cutlery and china crashing to the floor. But only if no one's home, of course."

"There's always someone home here," Sam said, closing his eyes as her hands lightly massaged the back of his neck. "That's the problem with being rich enough to have servants."

"I've got a kitchen table back in Connecticut," Ellen told him. "And a house that's absolutely servant-free."

Sam sat up a little straighter and opened his eyes. "Is that an invitation?"

She seemed almost taken aback by the direction the conversation had suddenly turned. "Well, I . . ."

"Because if it is, consider me there."

Ellen was honest. "Sam, I was just teasing. I don't expect you ever to visit me in Connecticut."

"Why not?"

She smiled crookedly and leaned forward to kiss him. "Be serious."

He pulled back before she could deepen the kiss and thoroughly distract him. "I am serious."

"Okay, then don't be serious."

Sam looked into her eyes, his heart in his throat. "But I want to be serious. For the first time in my life, I do want to be serious."

She looked directly into his eyes. "Sam. Don't. Please?"

"Why not?"

"Because it wouldn't work. You and me? Are you kidding?" Laughing breathlessly, Ellen pulled off of him. She climbed out of the Jacuzzi and wrapped herself in a towel.

He took a deep breath. "Look. Would it make a difference if I went back to school and got a college degree?"

She stared at him, amazement on her face. "What?"

"I've always sort of wanted to, and this is a good reason actually to do it. Then you wouldn't have to be, well, embarrassed by me and . . ." He shrugged. "I want to be with you, Ellen, and if that would make me more acceptable . . ."

She was staring at him as if he were some sort of alien beamed down from outer space. "You think I don't want to become involved with you because I'm embarrassed that you don't have a college degree?"

"I don't know. I mean, it sounds crazy now that I say it out loud, but I can't figure out why else you won't spend any time with me."

"How about because you're nearly ten

years younger than me?"

Sam laughed, but then stopped laughing as he realized she wasn't kidding.

"You were twelve years old when Lydia was born. When *you* were born, a man had already walked on the moon, the Beatles were on the verge of breaking up, and *Star Trek* had been off the air for years. You're a child," she continued.

"I *was* a child. I'm not anymore. I sort of thought you noticed."

"Ten years is too much of an age difference," she persisted. "I did it the other way around, with Richard. It didn't work."

"It wasn't your age difference that didn't work," Sam pointed out. "It was Richard who didn't work."

But she'd already turned away from him, shaking her head. "You're too young, and I'm much too vulnerable. When I'm with you, I can't resist you. And making love is so incredible, but then, afterwards, I feel terrible, because I want . . ." She broke off, then turned to look at him, not even trying to hide the tears that were brimming in her eyes. "I . . . care too much for you, and that's only going to hurt me in the long run. I can't do this."

Sam felt his heart clench. "Ellen —"

"Every time you kiss me, I think maybe I

can handle the summer affair thing — that I can keep myself distanced while we have a purely sexual relationship, but the truth is that I can't. I want more than that. I want to be with someone I know I'm going to grow old with."

"So what you're saying is it's not a matter of age differences. It's a matter of trust."

Ellen shook her head. "Sam, even if commitment were your middle name — and I think you'll be the first to admit that it's not — you'll still be all those years younger than me. The only thing I could ever absolutely trust is that someday you would leave me."

"What, just because I'm only twenty-seven and not thirty-six like you? That's really stupid — and insulting."

She flushed. "I didn't mean to insult you."

Sam took a deep breath. "What can I do to convince you that you're wrong?"

Ellen wrapped her towel more tightly around her as she sadly shook her head. "Nothing," she whispered. "You can't change how old you are, Sam. I've thought about it, and there's just no way this is going to work."

ELEVEN

"So, what's this audition for?" Sam asked Lydia, settling into the backseat of the taxi. He was wedged between both kids, who swore that unless they sat near a window, the cab ride would make them throw up.

"Some disgusting breakfast cereal that's loaded with sugar," she told him offhandedly. "It's nothing like the spot Mom is shooting today. Did she tell you about it?"

"Not much. Only that she had to be over there at six A.M.," Sam said with a yawn. He'd woken up at five-fifteen — in his own sorry, lonely bed — and escorted Ellen to the studio where the commercial was being filmed.

The internal security on the set had been extremely professional. That, along with the fact that Ellen had told him point-blank that his presence would seriously throw off her concentration, had prompted him to call two of Hyunh's security guards to replace him. He'd miserably sat out in the hallway until they arrived. After last night's one-on-one with the stalker, Sam was also fairly confident that he was wrong about Ellen being the man's target. It had to be Bob the creep was after. Although he wished that the letters had arrived with a name on the envelope so that he could be absolutely sure.

Still, after instructing the guards that Ellen was not, under any circumstances, to leave the studio until he arrived himself to pick her up after the shoot, Sam went back to the town house and crawled into bed, every inch of him aching.

His shoulder hurt like hell. And his feelings were pretty battered too. After last night Ellen didn't even want to be in the same room with him. He'd virtually told her that he loved her, and her response had been to ask him to leave her room. And now his mere presence in the studio was too distracting.

Sam spent a few hours feeling bad about that until he realized maybe — just maybe — that was a *good* sign. He was a distraction. That was better then being someone who was easily ignored, right?

By early afternoon he'd slept a few hours and spent another few hours trying to think up ways he could age ten years in the next day or so. But he had come to the conclusion that it was not going to happen, no matter what he did.

It was hard not to be depressed, particularly since his shoulder ached every time he so much as moved, and his heart ached like hell regardless of whether he moved or not.

He was still lying in bed when the phone rang. He'd scooped it up quickly, hoping against hope that it was Ellen, but it was only Hyunh, asking if he was feeling up to playing bodyguard for Lydia while she went on an audition. Ellen had given Lydia permission to go — provided that Sam accompany her.

Sam knew he should feel good about that. Ellen had asked for him specifically, and her request implied a certain amount of trust. But it was hard to feel good about anything when every part of him hurt.

Still, he'd showered and grabbed a cup of coffee from the kitchen and here he was, heading out to some audition for a commercial spot for some disgusting breakfast cereal, as Lydia so aptly put it.

"The commercial that Mom's doing today is absolutely awesome," Jamie told him. "It's for Airwalk sneakers, and she plays this tough commander of a starship, kind of like Sigourney Weaver in the *Alien* movies."

"They faxed the sides and a storyboard to the house last night," Lydia said. "It's *very* cool. They're going to add all these computer-animated space aliens to the scenes Mom's shooting today. From what I could tell, it's going to have this really dark *Blade Runner* look. She gets to wear this ultracool uniform." She sighed. "I am *so* jealous. She must be having *so* much fun right now, and lately *I* can't even get a callback."

"What happened to your face?" Jamie asked Sam. "Bad guys get you?"

"Actually, yeah," Sam admitted. "Yesterday I had a little run-in with someone who didn't like me very much."

"Did you win the fight and haul their butt to jail?" Jamie asked eagerly.

Sam laughed. "Not quite. But I consider the fact that they didn't succeed in smashing my head in to be something of a personal victory."

"Was it . . . the stalker?" There was trepidation in Lydia's brown eyes.

"Yeah, I think it might've been," Sam told her.

"Is that what you were talking to Mom about so late last night?" Jamie asked.

Sam froze, uncertain of what to say. "Um, well, yes, we did talk about that after I got home, yeah."

Lydia leaned forward to glare at Jamie across Sam. "Were you up all night again, sneaking around the house playing your stupid spy games? If you *ever* sneak into my room while I'm asleep, I swear I'll wring your scrawny neck."

"Yeah, you're just afraid I'll tell everyone that you snore louder than a chain saw."

"I do not!"

"Do too!"

"Do *not!*"

"Guys." Sam put up his hands. "Please."

"He sneaks around the house at, like, two o'clock in the morning pretending he's part of the *Mission: Impossible* team," Lydia complained.

"That's better than talking on the phone to Ginny in Connecticut, taking three hours to describe the way your saxophone teacher taps his foot when you play, pretending that he doesn't realize you're only fifteen years old — just because you have a crush on the guy."

Lydia squinted her eyes menacingly at her little brother. "I do *not!*"

"You do too." He imitated her, fluttering his eyelashes and sighing. " 'Oh, it's Casey Redmond. He's *so* cute.' " He broke character and gazed at his sister loftily. "Believe me, I know things. I hear things." Jamie folded his arms across his chest. "Most of the time the house is pretty quiet, but last night there was lots of movement. You were on the phone with Ginny from eleven-fifteen until one-thirty talking about Casey. Hyunh had some weird meeting with Bob after midnight, and I don't know *what* time that ended. And Sam was talking to Mom in her room until close to two A.M. . . ."

Hyunh and Bob? Sam had suspected there was something going on between the talk show host and his diminutive security chief. They'd no doubt had a "meeting" similar to the one Sam had had with Ellen. And Jamie, in his innocence, didn't realize the implications of such a late-night tryst.

But Lydia did. Sam glanced in her direction to find her staring at him, wide-eyed, her expression unreadable. She quickly looked down at her hands folded in her lap, then out the window. She knew he'd been with her mother last night, and Sam couldn't just pretend that she didn't know.

"So," he said brightly in the sudden uncomfortable silence. "I'm in love with your mother."

That brought Lydia's eyes back to his face. Jamie was clearly stumped at the apparent non sequitur.

"So, what do you guys think about that?" Sam added.

Lydia laughed nervously. "I had no clue."

"You and *Mom?*" Jamie's voice was tinged with disbelief. "Really?"

"Well, I don't know how she feels about me," Sam told the little boy, "but I'm definitely crazy about her."

Jamie nodded, as if that were to be expected. "She's pretty nice. And funny. She has a good sense of humor for a mom."

"God, you are *so* narrow-minded," Lydia leaned forward to shoot Jamie down. "She has a good sense of humor for a human being, do you mind?"

The cab stopped outside the casting agency's building. Sam peeled a five-dollar bill from his billfold and handed it to the driver, then followed Lydia out of the taxi.

"Are you going to move to Connecticut, or are we going to move to New York?" Jamie asked Sam, scrambling out after them onto the sidewalk.

"Well, I —"

"I *love* New York," Lydia said, starting for the door to the building. "I want to move to New York. Definitely."

"Whoa," Sam said. "Guys. Hang on a sec —"

"You don't love New York, you love Casey

Redmond," Jamie scoffed at his sister as they went inside the elevator. "I want to live in Connecticut. I mean, the city's okay, but I like to be able to go outside without a bodyguard." He gazed pensively at Sam as the doors opened on the third floor. "Although you'd be pretty bored if you were a police detective in our town. We don't have too many stalkers to worry about."

"Thank God." Sam followed them out of the elevator and past the reception desk, where a woman sat. She glanced briefly up at them as they passed. They'd been here before, and Sam knew where to go, but let Lydia lead the way. "Look guys, I think this conversation is a little pre—"

"Are you going to be our stepfather?" Jamie asked as Lydia signed in at one of the many tables in the wide hallway and took a script from the pile there. Sam glanced at the names above hers on the list — it looked as if there wouldn't be that long a wait. But then he realized what Jamie had said.

Stepfather?

"I saw this movie once where the stepfather tried to kill all the kids," Jamie continued, "but you wouldn't do that because you're a cop, right?"

"Oh my God, you and Mom are going to get married? That's so *cool!*" Lydia was beside herself, talking at the same time as Jamie. "I saw this great dress in *Seventeen* magazine that I could wear to the ceremony and —"

"Guys. *Guys!*"

Lydia and Jamie stopped talking for only a moment. They both blinked at him, then started right in again as he ushered them into several of the chairs set along the wall.

"You're not going to make us call you Dad, are you? I mean, we'll still be able to call you Sam, right?"

"You're going to love our house in Connecticut. We have this huge yard — it's great for playing baseball and soccer."

"We're getting a little ahead of ourselves here," Sam said loudly. "Your mother and I haven't exactly talked about marriage yet." Yet? What, was he nuts? He'd said "yet" as if the topic were on his list of things to discuss with Ellen in the near future.

"You haven't?" Jamie gazed at him owlishly from behind his glasses. "Well, gee, what are you waiting for?"

"Lydia Layne." A man held the clipboard today. Lydia stood up and he waved her toward the door.

"Wow, that was fast," Lydia said. "I didn't even get a chance to read the sides."

The man took the script from her hands.

"You won't need that, sweetie. Just go on in. Quickly now. The client's got PMS and it's a full moon — we're all a little pissy today."

"Break a leg," Sam and Jamie said in unison.

The door closed behind her.

Jamie stood up. "I'm going to get a drink. There's a water fountain right around the corner."

Sam nodded, sitting tiredly down, wincing as his shoulder hit the back of the chair. "Come back right away, all right?"

"You bet." Jamie sauntered off, and Sam leaned his head back, briefly closing his eyes. It was suddenly so peaceful without the kids around. Still, he found himself smiling. They were good kids, although he was going to have to break them of the habit they had of constantly sniping at one another. He'd worked for a few years as a Youth Officer, and he understood kids in their age group pretty well, and . . .

"Hey, where's Jamie?"

Sam opened his eyes to see Lydia standing in front of him, a frown on her pretty face.

He stood up. "He just went to get some water. You were quick."

"Yeah," she said glumly. "It was one of

231

those auditions where I looked into the camera, gave my name, rank, and serial number, they ordered me to turn to the left, turn to the right, and 'Thank you! Next.' "

They rounded the corner and there was one of those water coolers with cone-shaped paper cups in a metal dispenser alongside of it. But there was no Jamie.

"Oh my God," Lydia breathed. "Where did he go?"

Fear hit Sam hard in the gut. Where *did* the kid go? He knew enough not to just wander off. Sam spun around, searching for the little boy. He was wearing, what? A red T-shirt. That shouldn't be too hard to spot . . .

Sam took Lydia's hand and pulled her with him at a run toward the elevators. But there was no one over there either.

"Sir," the woman behind a reception desk said disapprovingly. "I must ask you please not to run."

"Did you see a little boy" — Sam nearly vaulted over the reception counter — "about ten, brown hair, blue eyes, glasses? Red T-shirt?"

The woman backed away from him in alarm. "The boy who came in with you? No. He hasn't been back this way."

He pulled out his badge, nearly throwing

it at her. "NYPD." He moved back down the hall, calling over his shoulder, "Call 911, tell 'em Detective Sam Schaefer needs backup at this address."

The woman stared at him.

"Do it!" he shouted, and she reached for the phone.

"Oh my God," Lydia said again, tears in her eyes. "Do you think Jamie's been kidnapped?"

"Stay close to me," Sam ordered, unable to answer her question. "I don't want to lose you too."

A group of African-American men were waiting outside one of the doors, all dressed similarly in athletic clothes, all tall enough to be college basketball players.

"I'm looking for a missing kid," Sam told them, talking fast. "Ten years old, red T-shirt, glasses, brown hair. I'm a detective with the New York police, and I have reason to believe he's just been kidnapped, but he's still somewhere in this building. Will you help me look for him? Brown hair, glasses, red T-shirt," he repeated as the men nodded, then moved off in different directions.

One of the women holding a clipboard had overheard him, and he turned to her now. "Where are the stairs heading down?"

The woman's eyes were wide. "Over by

the elevators."

Sam shook his head. Jamie hadn't been back that way. "Any others? Back staircases, fire escapes?"

She pointed. "Down the hallway, to the left. There's a window with a fire escape."

Lydia was crying in earnest now, and Sam took her hand again and started to run. She was slowing him down, but he didn't dare leave her. No way was he going to lose both of Ellen's kids. Losing Jamie was bad enough.

He pushed his way through the hallway, taking a left at the end, and there it was. The window. It was open wide despite the building's air-conditioning, and he felt sick.

The psycho who'd made those awful phone calls, who'd drawn those terrible pictures, who'd tried to kill him last night, had taken Ellen's precious child.

He let go of Lydia's hand and leaned out the window, praying that he wasn't too late, praying that he'd see the man still carrying the boy down the fire escape or running in the alley below. But there was no one out there. They were long gone.

He'd failed.

Again.

"Hey!" A cry came from the other side of the room. "Hey, over here! We found him!

The little boy! He's in the men's room!"

The men's room?

Sam stared at Lydia.

"I'm going to *kill* him," she said through clenched teeth, wiping her tear-streaked face on her sleeve.

"Not until after *I* kill him," Sam told her, starting back through the crowded hallway.

"Hey! Detective! You better come quick!" There was urgency in the voice that was calling, and Sam grabbed hold of Lydia's arm one more time and broke into a run.

Curious people had gathered outside of the men's room, and one of the tall black men frowned at them. "Yo. Here comes the man. Let him through."

The crowd parted obediently.

"Is he all right?" Sam asked, a new blade of fear stabbing into his gut at the grim look on the man's face.

"As far as I can see. But he's tied up with tape across his mouth."

"What?"

"Come see."

Sam pulled Lydia with him, right into the men's bathroom. And there was Jamie, sitting on the floor against the far wall. His hands and his feet were tied, his glasses dangled from one ear, and he was crying like a child half his age.

One of the basketball-tall actors was carefully worrying free the tape over the boy's mouth, and another was working to untie the rope that bound his ankles and wrists.

Both the rope and the tape came off as Sam knelt down next to Jamie, and he pulled the little boy into his arms. Jamie clung to him, sobbing.

Lydia was crying again, too, as she joined them on the floor, and Sam had to work hard to fight back his own tears of relief.

"He's got some kind of note taped to his shirt," one of the men told Sam. "Check it out. Whoever put this kid here was a real freak. Count your blessings that he didn't do more than tie the boy up."

Sam looked, and sure enough, there was a note taped to Jamie's chest. He pulled it free.

The aleens want death, it said. *They are watching me. More blood will flo soon. I am watching you.*

Aleens? Aleens? *Aliens.*

Holy God. Ellen was working on a commercial that had aliens. Had he been wrong after all? Was the stalker really still after Ellen?

A uniformed policeman came into the bathroom. "Sam? You in here?"

"Tommy." Sam's backup had arrived, and

it was an officer he knew well. "Get on the phone and call Tran Minh Hyunh at 555–8734. Tran Minh Hyunh, okay? Tell her to get over to Soundfire Studios on Fifty-seventh Street. Tell her to find Ellen Layne and not let her out of her sight. Then get on the phone to the precinct and get a squad car over there, too, right away."

"You got it, Detective." Tommy vanished.

Jamie's tears had begun to slow, and now he lifted his head, looking up at Sam.

"I saw him," the little boy said. "The guy who brought me in here and tied me up. I looked him straight in the eye." He wiped his nose with the back of his hand and took a deep, shuddering breath. "I could ID him, Sam. I *know* I could."

TWELVE

Ellen sat with her children until they fell asleep, side by side in the twin beds in Jamie's room. It was only ten o'clock, but they had clearly both been exhausted by the trauma of Jamie's run-in with the stalker.

Lydia had come into her brother's room, only intending to sit with them as Ellen stroked Jamie's hair and held him close, but she had curled up on the other bed and fallen asleep too.

It was all Ellen could do to keep from lying down on the carpeting between the two beds and falling into a deep, dreamless, fatigue-filled slumber herself.

It had been nearly six P.M. when Hyunh had arrived at the studio with the frightening news that although Jamie was safe, he'd been grabbed by the stalker. At the time, Ellen had already been working for nearly twelve hours, but the shoot was far from over.

The director had grudgingly allowed her to leave to go to her son, who was at the police station looking through books of mug shots hoping to recognize the face of his abductor. But the director had also made her promise that she would return to the studio at eleven the next morning for the remainder of her shots.

Ellen didn't want to go back. The entire shoot had been drastically different from the laundry detergent commercial she'd done with Lydia. Perhaps it was the absence of children on the set, or perhaps it was the style and personality of the director, who was a hard, rude, unforgiving man who used bad language and a raised voice to communicate his needs, of which there were many. Compared to the lightheartedness and laughter that were prevalent among the crew on the first commercial's set, this shoot was manned by a crew of grim, anxious, beaten-down people.

And without Lydia there to keep her company, the waiting was interminable. In between each shot the lights and camera had to be moved, and that took forever.

All in all, it had been an overwhelming day — including the phone call she'd received from her agent while on the set. She'd been offered a three-month contract with that new soap opera. Accepting the role would mean she'd have to give up her teaching position at Yale. But then what would happen if, in three months, her contract wasn't renewed?

She hadn't intended to tell the kids, but somehow Bob had found out and her secret was not so secret anymore. Added into the equation was the fact that Sam, damn him, had had the gall to say something to Jamie and Lydia that had led them to believe he and Ellen had a future together.

Ellen dragged herself down to the kitchen, in need of a hot cup of tea before she tucked herself into bed and turned out the light.

But Sam was in there.

She didn't notice him until she was halfway into the room, and by then it was too late to turn around and walk away.

She hadn't had to talk to him privately at the police station, and she had hoped to continue to avoid him. It was hard enough just being in the same room with him, but talking to him — looking into his eyes — that was torture. He thought he was in love with her. He'd been prepared to get a college degree because he'd thought that was what was keeping her from wanting to be with him.

It was hard not to be swayed by that.

Clearly, if he was intending to spend four years getting a degree, he had something a little longer term than a summer affair in mind.

But how stupid would she be to get involved — deeply, emotionally involved — with a man like Sam? While they were at the police station, she'd had an opportunity to see firsthand the kind of reaction he received from the female population.

Women watched him. Some covertly, some openly, obviously. With his charisma and his incredible good looks, he was, as Lydia might say, a babe magnet. In that way, he was so much like Richard, it was scary. And one heart-ripping betrayal per lifetime was all Ellen could stand.

"Bob tells me you have to go back to the studio tomorrow morning," he said, pouring himself a mug of coffee. He lifted the pot in her direction. "Want some? It's decaf."

He looked impossibly good in his rumpled white dress shirt and jeans. The scrapes and bruises on his face didn't look too bad, and his blond hair seemed to glisten in the dim light.

"I'm having tea, thanks," she told him.

"I think the water in the kettle's still hot. Let me get you a mug."

He winced as he reached up into the cabinet for another mug, and she knew that his shoulder still hurt him badly. She clenched her teeth to keep herself from asking how he was feeling. The less she said to him, the better.

"Is Jamie asleep?" he asked, handing her the mug.

She was careful not to let their fingers touch. "Yeah."

"He get a chance to tell you what happened?"

She nodded as she took a tea bag from the canister. "Yes. He went to get a drink of water and the man came up right behind him. The man showed his gun and said that if Jamie made any noise at all or tried to run away, he'd kill him. And then he'd kill you and Lydia. So Jamie went with him, into the bathroom, where the man tied him up."

Sam nodded too. "It was my fault," he said quietly. "Totally. Ellen, I can't tell you how sorry I am this happened."

Ellen found herself defending him. "Lydia told me her entire audition didn't take more than two minutes. It all happened so quickly."

But Sam was shaking his head. "I shouldn't have let him walk away from me.

I should have made him wait to get the drink of water until Lydia was back. I should have stayed with him."

"There was no way you could have known —"

"You're wrong," he said flatly. "I *should* have known. If I had been doing my job right, I *would* have known."

She leaned against the counter, as far away from him as she could possibly be while still standing in the same room. "You don't really believe that, do you?"

He pointedly changed the subject. "Congratulations, by the way, on being offered that soap opera role."

Ellen felt a flare of frustration. "Who told you about that?"

"Bob."

She exhaled in disgust. "Lord, that man can't keep a secret."

"Was it supposed to be a secret?" Sam asked.

"Yes, because I don't know if I'm going to accept the part. I wanted time to think about it without anyone pressuring me."

He was clearly surprised. "You're not going to take it? I thought this was what you wanted — a new career. Ellen, it's fallen right in your lap. How could you not accept the part?"

"That's exactly what I didn't want. Other people's opinions," she said hotly. "And speaking of not keeping secrets — what were you thinking? I can't believe you said something to Jamie and Lydia about our relationship. God, we don't even *have* a relationship!"

She saw a sudden flare of hurt in his eyes that he quickly tried to hide with a smile. "Look, I only told them the truth. That I'm crazy about you. I didn't see any harm in that."

"No? Lydia brought *condoms* to my room tonight," Ellen told him. "She gave them to me, along with a speech about safe sex."

He cringed. "Oh, damn, really?"

"Really. She told me she called the drug-store that delivers and pretended to be me. She ordered an entire box of them along with some shampoo and aspirin, and they just sent them on over."

Sam couldn't hide his smile.

"This isn't funny, Sam. Exactly how crazy about me did you tell Jamie and Lydia that you were?"

He took a sip of his coffee, gazing at her over the top of his mug, his expression suddenly unreadable. "Jamie saw me leaving your room last night."

Ellen swore softly.

"It could be worse," he pointed out. "At least they like me."

"Of course they like you. You're nearly as young as they are!"

"You know, I've been thinking about this a lot, Ellen, and frankly, that argument about our age difference doesn't cut it with me." He set down his coffee mug. "It's cowardly. It's an excuse not to confront the real issue here."

"I have to go." She tried to push past him, but his words stopped her cold.

"Go on. Run away. Again. The same way you're running away from this acting job. You say you want a change, but you don't really, do you? You won't take this job, you won't let yourself have a real relationship with me. You'll only allow yourself occasional physical gratification by having sex with me every now and then because you're scared that if you let this thing between us grow, I'll hurt you the way Richard did."

Ellen was silent. She couldn't deny it.

"This summer was supposed to be *your* time," Sam continued softly. "You were supposed to take chances, do things for yourself. But, babe, I've got to tell you, you're doing it all half-assed."

She turned to face him. "I'm doing the best I can." Her voice shook.

He shook his head. "No, you're not. You're quitting. Ellen, come on. Don't quit on me."

She couldn't say anything. She could only look into his eyes, trapped by the steady intensity of his gaze.

"You know, I was going to quit tonight," he said quietly. "I spent the entire evening at the precinct, staring at the suspect profile, hoping for some clue as to who this son of a bitch is, trying to make up for all of the mistakes I've made so far. I mean, we don't even know who he's after. Is it Bob? Or you? The reference to aliens in the note today made me think it's you, but I can't figure out how he found out you're shooting this commercial. Is he connected to someone in the crew? Does he work with your agent?"

Sam took a deep breath. "Really, what do we know about this guy? He has some artistic talent, his paranoid words imply some sort of delusional schizophrenia, and he has access to a fireman's mask and gear," he said, ticking them off on his fingers. "We know that despite his inability to spell, he was smart enough to plan ahead and disable the Cafe Allessandra's sprinkler system before his attack at the restaurant. We know he wasn't easily identifiable from the mug shot books that Jamie looked through, so it's possible he has no priors. We know from

Jamie's description that he's a medium-height, medium-weight Caucasian man with medium brown hair, about thirty years old. And — oh yeah — we know he has a gun."

He tiredly rubbed his face. "A police artist is going to come by tomorrow afternoon to work with Jamie to make a composite sketch — that's the earliest they could schedule it," he continued. "After that, I'll circulate the picture at your agent's office and with the crew at Starfire Studios. Maybe that'll help, maybe someone will recognize him, but probably not.

"So I'm sitting there, thinking about this, thinking it's pretty hopeless, thinking that I suck, thinking I should take myself off the case. Hell, you don't want me around, and I'm obviously not doing anyone else a whole lot of good either."

"But —" Ellen stopped herself. But what? This was what she wanted, wasn't it? For Sam to walk out the door and not come back? If he really wanted to be taken off the case, she shouldn't try to talk him out of it.

He took a step toward her, but then stopped himself as if he were afraid she would back away. "But if I just walk away, that would be quitting, and you know what I found out tonight as I was sitting there? I found out that I'm not a quitter. This job is tough, and sometimes, despite all of my best intentions, I make mistakes. You know, I almost didn't agree to take this case in the first place because three months ago I was assigned to protect a witness and — you know, I used to be unable to say this — but *due to circumstances beyond my control,* that witness nearly died."

He paused and she stood there silently, wanting to hear more.

"It was awful, Ellen. Four people were shot, and I watched it all happen, as if in slow motion. It was only sheer luck they didn't die — and it was touch and go for a while there." He took a deep breath. "After it was all over, I figured this is it. I can't do this anymore. I'm not good enough. I'm telling you, Ellen, my confidence was trashed. I actually thought I should've been able to foresee everything that could possibly go wrong. I thought I should have been able to second-guess the fact that a man I trusted — a police officer who had been with the force for thirty years — had been blackmailed into revealing the location of our safe house."

He paused, the intensity of his eyes keeping her from turning away. "But I kept putting off typing up a letter of resignation, because even though I'm not perfect, you know what? I *am* good at what I do. And the thought of giving up sets my teeth on edge.

"So I didn't quit. And I'm not going to quit now," he told her. "I'm not going to walk off this case, and I'm not going to walk away from you. Bottom line: I love you. God, I never thought I'd say those words, but there you have it. I can't break it down into anything simpler than that. I want to be with you. And you're just going to have to get used to me hanging around."

Ellen could almost believe him. Maybe she *did* believe him. Maybe he even believed himself. Maybe he really did think he loved her. But how long would it last? She wasn't willing to take the kind of risk involved in finding that out firsthand.

"What time do you need to be at your shoot in the morning?" he asked.

"Eleven."

Sam swore. "I've got a meeting scheduled at ten over at Bob's studio. My lieutenant's coming out to talk to him, and I have to be there. There's no way I can go to that and then get back here in time to get you to Starfire at eleven." He swore again. "Okay. I know. You're just going to have to come along with me to the meeting. We'll leave from there."

"That's ridiculous. I can go over with Hyunh."

"Nope. You go with me, or you don't go at all. No exceptions. I might make mistakes, but I don't make them twice."

"But Hyunh is one of the best bodyguards in the country."

"When it comes to your uncle, yeah, you're right, she is."

"Then I don't understand why —"

"If we're outside the house, then I'm next to you," he told her. "This is not something I'm going to change my mind about."

"But Hyunh has had even more experience than you in —"

"If it's Bob this guy's after, I wouldn't doubt for a moment that she would be the best person to protect him," Sam said.

Ellen didn't get it. "What's the difference?"

"You're not Bob. And I'm not so sure she'd throw herself in front of a bullet for you."

"And you would?"

He didn't say anything, but his answer was written all over his face. Yes. He would.

Ellen stared at him in shock. In the sudden silence, she could hear the ticking of Bob's grandfather clock in the living room. Nearly an entire minute seemed to pass before Sam shifted his weight and looked away from her.

"I wasn't kidding when I told you that I love you," he said quietly, glancing back into her eyes.

Ellen gazed back at him, unable to speak, barely able to breathe. She did the only thing she *could* do. She ran for her room.

THIRTEEN

There were suitcases in the entrance when Sam came downstairs in the morning.

The brawnier of the three muscle-bound security guards — Barney was his name — was by the front door. He glanced up at Sam and nodded a greeting.

"What's this?" Sam asked, afraid he already knew the answer to his own question.

"From what I understand, Ms. Layne and the kids are leaving tonight," Barney told him.

Sam nodded. "Can I get you a cup of coffee from the kitchen?" he asked, the even tone of his voice not betraying the turmoil brewing inside him.

Ellen was leaving. Tonight.

"Nah," Barney said. "I've had my caffeine today. But thanks."

Sam nodded again and went into the kitchen. There were bagels and cream cheese out on the counter, but he seemed to have lost his appetite.

As he poured himself a mug of coffee Ellen came into the room. She was wearing jeans and a T-shirt, and her hair was pulled back into a casual ponytail. She looked maybe seventeen years old at the most.

"Whoa," she said when she saw him. "Déjà vu. Weren't we just here?"

She was trying to be cheerfully nonchalant. It wasn't working.

Sam turned to face her. "So, when exactly were you planning to tell me you were leaving?"

Some of her forced cheerfulness vanished. But Ellen held her ground, even raising her chin as she met his eyes. "I wasn't keeping it a secret."

"It would've been nice if you had come to tell me, maybe even talked it over with me first."

"You would've tried to talk me out of it."

"Damn right I would've." He glanced at his watch, taking one last slug of his coffee before setting his mug down on the counter. "We've got to pick up T.S. on our way to Bob's office. We should probably get going."

He followed her out of the kitchen and down the hall. Barney opened the door for them and led the way down the front path toward the limousine waiting at the curb.

No one else was on the sidewalk. That was good. Still, they couldn't get inside the limo quickly enough to satisfy Sam. Ron opened the car door, and Sam nearly pushed Ellen inside, then climbed in himself.

"I think you're turning into an agoraphobic," Ellen complained, rubbing a bumped elbow.

"What I'm afraid of is a little more specific than open spaces," he told her. "I'm afraid of a shooter on a neighbor's roof. Or maybe someone driving by with a semiautomatic."

He'd sat down next to her, and now she moved so that she was sitting across from him, farther away.

Sam glanced out the window as the limo started rolling, well aware that they were mere minutes from T.S.'s house. If they were going to talk privately, he didn't have much time.

"So tell me, honestly, what are you running away from? The stalker? Or me?"

Ellen laughed nervously. "Wow, you really cut to the chase."

"You're leaving tonight. I don't have a lot of time to spend on small talk."

She could no longer meet his eyes. "I don't know what to say to you, Sam. You know where I stand on —"

"Yeah, you think I'm too young. That part

I know by heart. I don't understand it, but I know it. Why don't you start by telling me how you could make love to me the way you did two nights ago without feeling *some*thing."

She looked up at him then. "Oh, please. Don't pretend you've never had a relationship based purely on sex."

"You're right, I have. Too many times. But I don't think you ever have." He moved across the car so that he was sitting next to her again as the limo pulled up in front of T.S.'s building.

Sam glanced out of the window. He could see T.S. walking toward the limousine. He must've been waiting in the lobby. Ellen shifted, about to switch seats again, but he stopped her, holding her arm, gently forcing her to look at him.

"I love you," he told her softly. "We can make this work. Wherever you're going tonight, let me come with you and —"

The door opened and T.S. got in. Talk about timing.

"Hey, white boy," he greeted Sam jovially, then nodded at Ellen. "How are you, Ellen?"

"Fine," she said faintly.

"Me too," T.S. said, settling back in his seat. He had on his Cheshire Cat smile, and Sam knew that, as sensitive as his best

255

friend usually was, T.S. wasn't picking up the tension between Sam and Ellen. "I just received some really great news from my publisher. They're going wild with the publicity for my next book. It's coming out late October, and it has Christmas gift written all over it. The publisher is doing everything it can to promote it — and I mean *everything,* except maybe tying it in with a fast-food Happy Meal. I was starting to think they were cooling their jets with me, you know, pulling back on the publicity bucks because I wouldn't do the talk show circuit, but this is pretty huge. It's bigger than the effort they made for the alien book, three years ago. Remember that one?"

"*Alien Contact,*" Ellen said. "Yes. I think I remember seeing commercials on television for that one."

"That's right." T.S. was very happy.

Sam was not. "Ellen's leaving town tonight," he told T.S. flatly. "She's running scared — she's *quitting* — because she finally believes me when I tell her that I'm in love with her."

T.S. froze, glancing from Ellen to Sam. "Well. Gee. Maybe I should sit up front with Ron?"

Ellen closed her eyes. She should have known that Sam wasn't going to let her just slip away. She should have known that he would fight her decision to leave, that he would resist, kicking and screaming.

"And you know what the really stupid thing is?" Sam continued. He was talking to T.S. but looking at Ellen. "She loves me too."

Ellen closed her eyes. "Sam, I'm sorry if I've given you that impression."

T.S. shifted uncomfortably in his seat. "I think it would be a really great idea if I could just use the intercom or the phone or whatever you've got in this thing to talk to Ron so I can ask him to pull over and —"

"Look me in the eye," Sam demanded. "Come on, Ellen. I dare you. Look me directly in the eye and tell me you don't love me. 'I don't love you, Sam.' If it's true, you can say it, no problem, right?"

Ellen couldn't say it. She couldn't even look at him. "I don't *want* to love you, dammit!"

"Aha! Not the same thing. Right, Toby? You're an expert with words. 'I don't want to love you' is not even close to 'I don't love you,' wouldn't you say?"

"Oh, good," T.S. said as the limousine pulled to the curb. "We're here."

"Don't quit on me, Ellen," Sam told her.

The limo door opened and Ellen

scrambled out, wishing she were as strong as Sam believed her to be. But she wasn't, and it *was* easier to quit. It was far easier to walk away than to risk her heart.

Quitting now meant that she wouldn't have to wait around, in a permanent sense of dread, wondering when their affair would end.

Sam watched Ellen pull away from him, and he knew that he'd lost — not the war, just the battle. Ellen was going to find out that it would take more than that to make him walk away.

He squinted in the bright sunlight as he hustled Ellen and T.S. toward the entrance of the network building. The big lobby was open to the public, but it would be better than being out on the sidewalk. And once across the marble-tiled expanse, they would take one of the private elevators up to Bob's suite of offices.

The doorman pulled the doors open, and Sam scanned the lobby. The network had beefed up security — in addition to the man behind the desk barring general access to the elevators, there were three armed guards at the door and three others positioned around the room. He also spotted two undercover detectives from his own precinct — clearly, after yesterday's incident with

Jamie, his lieutenant was finally taking the threats seriously.

A few dozen other people were around, some looking at the artwork on the walls, some hanging out in the air-conditioned coolness of the lobby hoping to get passes to Bob's afternoon taping, some waiting to meet other people — glancing at their watches or reading a newspaper.

One of them, a man with a folded newspaper under his arm, started to cross the lobby, his pace and his route on a direct intercept course with them. There was something odd about him, something about his body language, something about the way he was holding that newspaper.

The man glanced up and looked directly at Sam, and everything clicked into sharp focus.

"T.S. Harrison?" the man said.

Alien Contact. Three years ago T.S. had released a book called *Alien Contact.* Suddenly it all made perfect sense. The stalker wasn't after Bob or Ellen or even Lydia or Jamie. All this time, the stalker had been after *T.S.*

Sam reached for his gun, but he was too damn late.

As if in slow motion, he watched the newspaper fall away, revealing the man's gun. He heard himself shout for Ellen and T.S. to get down as it seemed to take an eternity to pull his own sidearm from his shoulder holster. He pushed Ellen down as the first of the bullets blasted into him, the roar of the gun echoing. He felt the impact, felt the searing, white-hot pain in his chest as he was pushed back, nearly on top of T.S.

A second and then a third bullet punched into him just as hard, and Sam knew in that instant he was a dead man, his future shrunk into the few short minutes it was going to take him to bleed to death right there on the white marble tile of the network lobby.

But he wasn't dead yet, and this bozo had three more bullets left in his gun — and Sam was damned if he was going to have the chance to use them on Ellen or T.S. With a strength he didn't know he had, he managed to pull his own gun free, and fired. Through a haze of pain and confusion, he seemed to see the gunman fall, but he wasn't certain.

He could hear people shouting; he could see T.S. kneeling beside him. He reached up and grabbed T.S.'s shirt. "Did I get him?"

"You did." T.S. was breathing hard as he

took the gun from his hand. "He's dead, Sam."

"Thank God." Sam fought the pain, struggling to sit up, to find Ellen, to assure himself she was all right. He turned, and Ellen was there. Ellen with her beautiful eyes. She was covered with blood. His blood, he realized, after a flash of panic. That was *his* blood. God, he didn't want to die. "I love you," he told her.

She was crying, he realized, her face wet with tears.

"An ambulance is coming, buddy," T.S. told him. "Just hang on."

"No time," Sam gasped. God, it was hard to breathe. One of the bullets must've hit one of his lungs. He had to get to a hospital, and he had to get there *now.* It was his only hope. "Help me. Now. The limo . . ."

Ellen was there, helping him up. "Help us," she said sharply to T.S. "Please! We'll drive him to the hospital ourselves!"

T.S. pulled Sam into his arms like a baby, carrying him back out to the street, to the limo.

The pain was nearly unbearable, but that pain meant he was still alive. Sam half crawled and was half dragged into the limo. Ron hit the gas before the door was even closed, lurching out into the street, tires squealing.

God, there was no time. He was so *cold* . . .

"Ellen?"

"I'm here, Sam." She was cradling him in her arms, trying to protect him from the jarring movement of the limo as it sped and bounced over potholes, racing toward the hospital. "I'm right here."

"Whatever happens, it's okay, because I was happy, being with you, you know?"

T.S.'s voice was raised and laced with fear. "Come *on,* Ron. Dammit! Can't you make this thing go any faster?"

"Don't you quit, Sam," Ellen told him. "I love you. Don't you quit on me now."

The limo bounced as they skidded to a stop in front of emergency room doors.

"Knew it," Sam whispered, somehow managing to smile as he fought the blackness, as he clung to the vision of her beautiful face. "Knew you loved me too."

Ellen prayed. She sat in the church chapel as the hours ticked slowly past.

Hyunh had brought her a change of clothes. She couldn't remember going into the ladies' room and changing, but she must have, because she was wearing a clean pair of jeans and a different T-shirt.

Her other clothes had been nearly saturated with Sam's blood.

He was in surgery now, his life in the hands of the doctors and God. Ellen could do nothing but wait. And hope that he'd heard her when she'd told him not to quit.

But he wasn't the quitter.

She was.

Sam could feel the painkillers coursing through his system before he even tried to open his eyes. His eyelids were incredibly heavy, and his mouth tasted like crap, and it would've been a whole hell of a lot easier just to sink back into unconsciousness, except someone was holding his hand.

He knew that someone had to be Ellen, and he knew if he could only get his damned eyes open, he'd see her gorgeous smile.

Don't quit, she'd told him.

Well, he hadn't quit yet.

He opened his eyes and found that it wasn't going to be that simple. He had to work to bring his vision into focus, and even after he did, he still didn't see Ellen.

He moved his head to look down at his hand, and there she was. She'd pulled a chair next to him, and she'd fallen asleep, her head resting on his bed.

He pulled in a breath to speak — bad idea. His words came out as a groan of pain, but it got the job done. She lifted her head, pushing her hair back from her face.

"Sam?"

He didn't breathe quite so deeply this time. "Hey, babe," he said, nearly soundlessly.

She started to laugh and cry, both at the same time. "I better call the nurse."

"Are you kidding? I don't want to kiss the nurse — I want to kiss *you*."

She pushed the call button anyway, then leaned over him, gently brushing his lips with hers.

"The doctor says you're going to be all right," she told him.

"Told you I don't quit."

Ellen squeezed his hand. "I've decided not to quit either." She smiled at him. It was the most beautiful thing he'd ever seen. "Because you were right."

Sam forced his eyes open a little wider, but he felt more of the painkiller kick in and he knew it was a losing fight.

She took a deep breath. "I was wondering if maybe, in September, you would, um, consider relocating to Connecticut. You see, I'm not going to stay in New York. I don't want that soap job. I *really* don't want it,

Sam — it's not just because I'm afraid of change. I liked acting when I was working with Lydia — that's what made it fun. Being with my daughter. But when Lydia wasn't there, it was tedious. It's all waiting around and . . . I'm babbling because I just virtually asked you to move in with me, and maybe what you had more in mind was going out to dinner."

Move in with Ellen. *Move in* with *Ellen.* Hell, he didn't need the painkiller. He only needed to hear her say things like that and he was filled with euphoria.

"Yes," he said. "Connecticut. Yes." It was an effort for him to get the words out, but he was rewarded by another soft kiss.

He closed his eyes, letting himself drift back into sleep, his future stretching out ahead of him like some endless shining road.

Connecticut. *Yes.*

"This," T.S. said emphatically, looking down at Sam, still plugged into all kinds of machines and tubes, "is definitely a reason to keep avoiding all those talk show invitations."

"You remember back in seventh grade when Eben O'Hara fired that spitball at me and it hit you right in the face?" Sam asked.

"Yeah?"

"Well, now we're even."

"Yeah, right. I take a spitball for you, you take three bullets for me? I owe you more than you could possibly know, my friend."

"What have you heard about this guy, this psycho, Geoffrey what's-his-name?"

"Whittier. Geoff Whittier."

"One of the detectives who searched his apartment came to see me yesterday, but I was still pretty out of it," Sam told his friend. "I have this vague memory of him telling me that this guy's place was unreal — something about him painting those freaky pictures on his walls?"

"Yeah," T.S. said. "I had a chance to read some of his journal entries. Sick stuff. He actually thought that aliens could speak to him. I'm guessing he was severely paranoid schizophrenic — hearing voices."

"Voices that told him to kill you because you wrote a book that gave equal time to the people who discount alien abductions."

"He had it in for me," T.S. said soberly. "Apparently he'd been waiting around for *years* for the chance to find me and blow me away."

"And what was this Whittier guy's connection to . . . was it Bob's limo driver?"

"Okay," T.S. told him. "You paying attention? Geoffrey Whittier lived next door to

Ron's — Bob's limo driver's — brother-in-law. His wife's brother."

Sam ticked off the connection on his fingers. "You're kidding."

"Andy — that's Ron's brother-in-law — he said that this Geoffrey Whittier came over to his apartment all the time. So he was there when Ron's wife called, all excited because Ron had met T.S. Harrison — which was really you."

Sam closed his eyes. "Oh, man."

"Ron's wife described you to her brother, who then told Geoffrey what T.S. Harrison supposedly looked like."

"Blond hair," Sam said. "Right?"

"You saw those pictures. That was supposed to be *you,* white boy." T.S. shook his head. "Pretty sick stuff."

There was commotion at the door, and Sam turned to see Ellen coming inside, along with Lydia and Jamie.

"They moved you!" Jamie announced. "Mom thought at first that maybe you died."

"I did not," Ellen exclaimed. Still, she came over and gave him an extremely heartfelt kiss. "You're out of intensive care."

He smiled at her, lacing his fingers with hers, tugging her down until she was sitting on the edge of his bed. "I am."

"How exciting! You look wonderful."

"Are you kidding?" Jamie interrupted. "Sam, God, you look *awful!*"

Lydia smacked her brother on the top of his head.

"Ouch! But he *does.*"

"You should've seen me a week ago," Sam told the little boy.

"Well, I didn't." Jamie sniffed, insulted. "They wouldn't let me."

"They didn't want your nasty little boy germs to infect him," Lydia told her brother, who pointedly ignored her.

"I got my class schedule for September," Jamie told Sam. "I got Mr. Brooks for homeroom. He's a total pain in the —"

"I can't believe we got our class assignments already," Lydia lamented. "I mean, come on. The summer's not even half over. It's not like we're going back to Connecticut for at *least* another month."

Connecticut. Yes.

Sam squinted, trying to focus on a very hazy memory. Was it possible? "Did you ask me to move to Connecticut with you?" he blurted out, unable to hold his question in.

Dead silence. Both Jamie and Lydia were struck silent, and Sam knew from the look in Ellen's eyes that this was perhaps not the wisest time to bring up the subject. Still, he had to know, right that moment. "You did, didn't you?"

T.S. stood up. "How about I take Jamie and Lydia down to the cafeteria for an ice cream or something."

"No way," Jamie said. "I want to hear this."

"Me too," Lydia echoed. "I mean, if Mom is thinking about getting remarried —"

Ellen was enormously embarrassed. "Nobody said anything about getting married." She could feel Sam watching her, feel his gaze on her face, and she glanced at him apologetically. "I'm sorry," she murmured.

"Nobody said anything about getting married because the last time we talked about it, I wasn't able to think very clearly," he told her.

Ellen glanced up, aware that T.S. was gently but firmly leading her children out of the room. He shut the door tightly behind them.

"I'm not remembering a hallucination, am I?" Sam asked. "You *did* ask me to come to Connecticut?"

She nodded. "Sam, I'm not going to hold you to something you said while you were —"

"I'm going to assume that you don't want me to come to Connecticut so that you can adopt me."

She snorted, trying to hide her smile. "You think you're too funny, don't you?"

"I *know* I'm funny — because I've managed to make you laugh even though we're talking about the dreaded M-word."

Ellen took a deep breath. "I was thinking we could maybe start out slowly — you with your own apartment and —"

"Do you love me?" he asked.

She closed her eyes and sighed. "You know that I do."

"Then marry me."

Ellen sat very still. She loved this man. It was fear that kept her from saying an immediate yes. Fear that he'd hurt her the way Richard had. But he *wasn't* Richard, he was Sam. Sam, who made her feel alive and ageless with his sparkling humor and quick wit. Sam, who'd fought tooth and nail against death itself to stay with her. Sam, who didn't quit — who would *never* quit.

She'd nearly lost him for good a week ago. The doctor had been bluntly honest in saying that only his good health, his youth, and his tenacious will to live had kept him alive. Ellen had had to laugh when Sam, too, had pointed out that an older man probably wouldn't have survived.

She opened her eyes and looked at him.

He looked impossibly cute sitting there with his hair tousled and the golden glint of a two-day-old beard on his chin.

"All right," she said.

"All right," he repeated softly. He smiled at her crookedly. "Well, all right, then." He pulled her closer for a soft, lingering kiss. "Now that we're engaged, am I allowed to call you babe?"

Ellen laughed. "Not a chance."

EPILOGUE

Sam pulled Ellen with him into the limousine waiting outside the church.

A freshly opened bottle of champagne waited for them, and Sam had to smile as he poured his wife a glass. His *wife.* His smile widened.

"Here's to traffic jams," he toasted, and she laughed.

She was gorgeous in her wedding dress. It was an eggshell white 1930s-style gown, cut low in the front and slit up the side to reveal flashes of her incredible legs. Sam couldn't believe it when he looked at the back of the church and saw her walking down the aisle, toward him.

He'd been totally turned on — which, oddly enough, was a nice addition to the joy and emotional excitement he was feeling at finally making Ellen his wife. At least it had been nice for the first hour and a half. But it was getting to the point where he was finding it extremely difficult to think about much else besides where and when they'd get a chance to consummate the vows they'd just made.

The photographer had had them posing for pictures for an interminable length of time, and now they were heading to their reception at Bob's house — a relatively small gathering of family and friends held upstairs in the elegant ballroom.

Sam kissed Ellen and she seemed to melt in his arms. Oh, man, the combination of this dress on this woman was killing him.

"Do you know how much I want you?" he asked huskily.

She pulled back to look into his eyes. "Do you know how much I want you?"

He kissed her again, weighing all of their options. "Do you think we can cut out of the reception early?"

"How early?"

"Like, after about five minutes?"

Ellen laughed. "I don't think so. Maybe after a couple of hours . . ."

He kissed her neck, her collarbone, the luscious tops of her breasts. "I have an idea. The party's up on the fifth floor, right? We have to take the elevator, right?"

Ellen laughed. "Are you suggesting we . . . ?"

He lifted his head and gazed into the glowing warmth of her eyes, giving her his most convincing smile. "You told me you always wanted to."

"Yeah, but not while seventy-five of our closest friends wonder why it's taking us so long to travel only several hundred feet!"

"Ellen, I'm *dying* . . ."

Ellen gazed into her husband's eyes and smiled. She picked up the phone and buzzed the driver. "Hi, Ron? Do you think you could take the long way — the *really* long way — home?"

Sam smiled and kissed her.

ABOUT THE AUTHOR

Since her explosion on to the publishing scene more than ten years ago, **Suzanne Brockmann** has written over forty books, and is now widely recognized as one of the leading voices in romantic suspense. Her work has earned her repeated appearances on the *USA Today* and *New York Times* bestseller lists, as well as numerous awards, including Romance Writers of America's #1 Favorite Book of the Year — three years running in 2000, 2001, and 2002 — two RITA awards, and many *Romantic Times* Reviewer's Choice Awards. Suzanne lives west of Boston with her husband, Dell author Ed Gaffney. Visit her website at www.Suzanne Brockmann.com.